THE BARONET'S WEDDING ENGAGEMENT

With his sister Hope about to marry a real-life prince, Max must find a suitable woman to partner with for the official engagement ball in San Michele. Flora Deare, Hope's friend and bridesmaid, is in charge of catering the royal wedding, and has quickly taken over Max's kitchen — not to mention the rest of his life. They decide to temporarily pose as a couple to keep the protocol-obsessed royals happy. A little pretence can't do any harm . . . can it?

JESSICA HART

THE BARONET'S WEDDING ENGAGEMENT

Complete and Unabridged

LINFORD
Leicester

First published in Great Britain in 2017

First Linford Edition
published 2019

*A catalogue record for this book is available
from the British Library.*

ISBN 978–1–4448–3968–5

Published by
F. A. Thorpe (Publishing)
Anstey, Leicestershire

Set by Words & Graphics Ltd.
Anstey, Leicestershire
Printed and bound in Great Britain by
T. J. International Ltd., Padstow, Cornwall

This book is printed on acid-free paper

1

'*How* long did you say you were moving in for?'

Max Kennard dumped the last box on the table and looked around him in dismay. The kitchen had been built at the back of the Tudor house by his great-great-grandfather, Sir Ralph Kennard, who had conveniently married an American heiress and proceeded to spend all her money on improving Hasebury Hall so that she could entertain in the style to which he fully intended to become accustomed. The kitchen itself was a grand, high-ceilinged room with tall windows looking out over the walled kitchen garden, and had a warren of sculleries, pantries and servants' quarters leading off it.

A great pine table, worn smooth by generations of cooks, stood in the middle of the room, and the original dresser

1

was ranged against one wall, but everything else had been spanking new thirteen years ago, when Georgie, Lady Kennard, had thrown money away on a major refurbishment while her husband, Max's father, was busy bankrupting the family.

So there were units and worktops aplenty, and that morning the kitchen had been an austerely spacious room, largely empty save for the microwave and toaster, which was all the cooking equipment Max required.

No longer. Now, every surface was cluttered with boxes and bags stuffed with every conceivable kitchen gadget. There were beaters and bowls, piping bags and peelers, graters and more different shapes of baking tins than Max had ever imagined. There were wickedly sharp-looking knives and food processors and saucepans. There were weird ingredients Max had never heard of, and plastic boxes and industrial-size rolls of greaseproof paper and foil. On the floor and chairs stood more boxes full of more spilling packing paper that his two dogs, Bella and Ted, were tearing apart with much growling.

And in the middle of it all stood Flora Deare, unpacking a complicated-looking machine from a box. 'I know it looks bad,' she said soothingly, 'but I'll only be here until June. Seven months, and all this will be gone, I promise.'

'It's going to take you seven months to put all this stuff away,' said Max with a dour look around. It wasn't that he spent any time in the kitchen, but the chaos made him uneasy.

'What's *that*?' he added suspiciously as she hoisted the machine out of its packing with a grunt. He could see lots of chrome, lots of fiddly bits.

'This? This is my most treasured possession,' Flora told him, giving whatever it was an affectionate pat. 'This is what gets me through the day. In short, it is a coffee maker.'

A coffee maker! Max barely restrained a snort. 'I've got one of those already,' he said. 'It's called a kettle.'

Flora rolled her blue eyes and tsked. 'Let me make you a real coffee. You'll never drink instant again.'

'I haven't got time to fuss around with fancy coffee,' he grumbled. He'd already wasted half the morning helping her carry in all the stuff from a van she had hired to bring her equipment out of storage.

'It won't take long,' said Flora. 'Besides, we need to talk about how things are going to work over the next few months, and you'll be less cranky if you sit down and have a coffee.'

'I'm not cranky,' Max said, crankily. He just had a perfectly reasonable dislike of having his home taken over and his well-ordered life turned upside down.

'Right.' Flora nodded, but he was outraged to see that a smile was tugging at the corners of a mouth that already seemed predisposed to tilt upwards. Was she *laughing* at him?

'Look, it really won't be so bad,' she said, as she dug around in a bag,

4

muttering to herself about coffee beans. 'I'll put all this away and clear the surfaces every night. You'll hardly know that I've been here.'

Max doubted that very much. Before they retired, her grandparents had run the shop and post office and, like them, Flora knew everybody. She was a striking figure, tall and lusciously curved and always animated. Since she had come back to look after her frail grandfather, Max had often noticed her laughing in the pub, or engaged in an intense conversation on the village green or leaning out of her car to banter with the postman.

And now she had taken over his kitchen, and Max was unsettled in a way he couldn't really explain. She was too vivid, too sociable. Her eyes were too blue. She charged the chilly air of the manor just by standing there, fiddling with that stupid machine. Max didn't like it, but it looked like he was stuck with her for the next few months.

'Do you really need all this . . . ' He

gestured around his kitchen. ' . . . all this stuff?'

'I might not,' said Flora, calmly pouring water into the coffee machine. 'I won't know until I've planned the menu for the wedding.'

Ah yes, the wedding. His sister's wedding. His sister's *royal* wedding. Had he mentioned the fact that Hope was going to be a princess? Oh, and that instead of marrying in the splendour of the royal palace in San Michele, like any normal princess-to-be would do, she had decided on a wedding in her childhood home.

'Jonas and I want a simple, intimate wedding,' Hope had said.

A simple, intimate royal wedding. Like *that* was going to happen. Max shook his head at the thought.

'We want to be married in St Philip and All Angels, and then walk back to a reception in the garden here. *Please* say we can, Max!'

How could he refuse her? Max was all too aware of the tough time his sister had had. He hadn't been able to save her from the effects of their father's stupidity and greed, but he was head of the family now, and if Hope wanted to get married at Hasebury Hall, that was what she would do, even if it bankrupted him all over again. Max had just struggled out from under the burden of debt their father's death had left on the estate, and he didn't want to think about how much a wedding, let alone a royal one, would set him back, but this was his sister. He would make it work somehow.

'I don't want you to be out of pocket because of this, Max,' Hope had said firmly as if reading his mind. 'Jonas is *disgustingly* rich, and he can afford a wedding. It's not as if we want anything grand or over the top, anyway, and we certainly don't want to spend our time arguing about the colour of the tablecloths. I've planned enough weddings to know that mine is going to be small and simple, so I've asked Flora to do the catering; and Ally's going to keep the press at bay, I hope; and all the flowers and the cake will be local. All you have to do is make the gardens look wonderful, which they do anyway. Oh, and to give me away, of course.'

Hope's smile had a painful edge that stuck the jokey retort he'd planned in his throat. Because Hope had always been a daddy's girl, and she must surely have dreamed of Gerald Kennard walking her up the aisle one day. Whenever he thought of his father, Max had to wrestle down a surge of rage and grief. How much had Gerald missed thanks to the stupidity and greed that had put him in prison before kidney disease had killed him?

How much was Hope still missing?

Max wasn't much given to hugging and kissing, but he put his arms around his sister then and held her close. 'I'm not sure I want to give you away,' he managed as she clung to him and buried her face in his shoulder. His throat was so tight he could hardly speak. 'I think I'd rather keep you. But if you will insist on throwing yourself away on the first prince who comes your way, I suppose I'll have to learn to live with it.'

Hope laughed a little shakily as she pulled herself from his embrace. Her green eyes, so like his own, were suspiciously bright, and she swiped a knuckle under them.

'Jonas is worth it,' she assured him.

So Max didn't care how much money His Serene Highness Prince Jonas of San Michele had. He was giving his sister her wedding. He couldn't replace her beloved father, but he could make sure that as far as her wedding was concerned at least, her dreams would come true.

'Don't worry about the cost,' he had said to Hope before she left.

Easy to say, not quite so easy to put into practice.

'We should really talk about how the next seven months is going to work,' Flora said, jerking him out of a morose memory of evenings spent staring at his latest bank statement, his only strategy being the hope that if he glared hard enough at it, the figure at the bottom would magically acquire some more zeros.

'Must we?' he said without enthusiasm. 'I thought we'd agreed. You use this kitchen until the wedding for your catering business, and in return I get a Michelin-starred chef to cater the wedding at a cut price.'

It was humiliating that Flora Deare knew how little he could afford, but ever since his father's trial and imprisonment had made national headlines, Max had learnt to live without pride. He might be Sir Max Kennard of Hasebury Hall, but nobody cared any more about the generations of Kennards who had looked after the land and the village, or the famous gardens that Max had lovingly preserved. He was just the son of Sir Gerald, naïve fool or corrupt fraudster, depending on your point of view, who had died in prison before he could try and sort out the mess he had created. And while Max might have been able to hold on to the house, everybody knew the rest of the family assets had had to be sold. He couldn't afford to be proud. Flora hadn't been crass enough to say as much when she put her proposition to him, but she hadn't needed to.

'Oh, and you're cooking every Thursday when Holly and Ben are here,' he reminded Flora, who gave him a wry look.

'I hadn't forgotten. You drive a hard bargain!'

'You shouldn't have told me how badly you needed the space,' said Max, unrepentant.

'It's true, though,' she said. 'You try supplying local cafés and restaurants with cakes, pies and pastries in my grandmother's tiny kitchen! I'd got to the point where I'd have done anything for more space. If I'd been able to rent a temporary kitchen, I wouldn't have had to impose on you, but at least catering Hope's wedding means we both get something out of the deal.

'And it's not as if it's a problem to cook for you and the kids occasionally,' she went on frankly. 'I've heard so much about them from Hope. I'm looking forward to meeting them. And in the meantime, it'll make such a difference having all this room to work in.' She looked around the kitchen with satisfaction.

Max followed her gaze, unable to see what was so pleasing about the clutter of boxes and bags. The kitchen looked a mess to him. Not that he came in here much. When Holly and Ben came over, he tried to make an effort to cook healthier meals, but it was all too tempting to fall back on pizza — tomatoes and mushrooms were vegetables, right? — while for himself, he was just as happy with beans on toast.

'Well, I'm glad it's working out for both of us,' he said after a moment.

'You might want to talk about a budget,' Flora started, but he held up a hand.

'No, I don't. I don't want to know about anything! I want you to cook whatever Hope wants and give me the bill.'

She gave him a disapproving look over her shoulder. 'That's a bit rash of you, isn't it?'

'You're one of Hope's closest friends,' said Max. 'She trusts you with a big part of her wedding, and that's good enough for me. Besides, I have no idea what I'm talking about when it comes to cooking, catering, weddings, or any of it. Use whatever ingredients you need and let me have a round figure. As far as I'm concerned, I'm getting the best part of the deal.'

Or so he'd thought when Flora had come round the previous Friday to put her proposition to him. But now here she was in his kitchen and suddenly it didn't seem such a good idea. He had just managed to restore order to his world after the twelve years of chaos that had begun with his father making national headlines then dying four years later in prison, and had continued with a bankrupt estate, his mother's death, the birth of his two children and finally divorce from Stella six years ago. Max felt he was due some quiet time, but there was nothing quiet about Flora.

He eyed her as she fiddled with the coffee machine. Today she was wearing jeans and a tight-fitting red jumper that accentuated her generous curves and made her look like a flame against the cold Victorian kitchen. She was just making coffee, Max knew, but she was changing things by standing there.

'How do you take your coffee?' She smiled at him over her shoulder and Max had the alarming sensation that the tiles had tipped abruptly beneath his feet. He could do without this kind of disturbance, he sighed inwardly, but if it would give Hope the wedding she wanted, then he would have to put up with it.

Resigned, he moved a box of platters from a chair and sat at the table. 'Black,' he said.

★   ★   ★

She might have known Max Kennard wouldn't go for a frothy cappuccino. She had never met anyone so resolutely unfrivolous. His face was set in stern lines, and he had an aloof air that befitted a baronet and the latest in a long line of Kennards at Hasebury Hall. According to Hope, who adored her brother, he was quite different when you got to know him. Like everyone else in the village, Flora knew Max had had to put up with a lot, but she couldn't imagine ever breaking through that intimidatingly starchy manner.

There was more than a touch of Mr Rochester in Max, Flora reckoned — minus the mad wife in the attic, of course. Tired of scraping by, Stella, Max's wife, had divorced him and remarried, and was now living on the other side of Ayesborough with the two children. Max lived alone in the great Tudor house his ancestors had built, sadly now emptied of all its treasures.

Sir Gerald's scandal and his death eight years earlier had left his son with crushing debts; Max had sold most of the estate, the paintings, the silver and all the valuable furniture, but against the odds he had been able to keep the manor intact.

Not that it seemed to give him any pleasure. He was glowering around the kitchen while she made the coffee. Maybe it *was* a bit of a mess, but she had only just arrived. He'd feel better after a coffee, Flora told herself.

She should make an effort, too. They were going to be spending the next few months together, after all.

'I can't tell you how relieved I am to have somewhere to cook properly,' she told him as she put the cup and saucer in front of him with a flourish, and went back for her own cappuccino. 'I'm longing to get started on Hope's menu.'

Pulling out a chair, she sat down opposite him. 'The kitchen is absolutely wonderful,' she said. 'I had a poke around earlier, and the larder is *fabulous*! It's got the original marble shelves.'

When Max just looked across the table at her with a sardonic expression which indicated that marble shelves left him cold, Flora found herself burbling on. 'I love the scullery too. Can't you just imagine the poor maids washing up in there?'

Of course, Max's ancestors wouldn't even have known where the scullery *was*, she remembered. Clearly they weren't going to bond over the kitchen. 'Anyway, the space is fantastic,' she said, and she spread her hands expressively as she looked around the kitchen. 'This is my fantasy,' she confided with a smile.

His brows lifted — and wait, was that the ghost of a smile she could see hovering about his mouth? It lightened the severe lines of his face, and Flora was abruptly aware of him: of the autocratic nose, the firm jaw, the green eyes glinting with mockery.

'It's not much of a fantasy, if you

don't mind me saying so.'

Ridiculously flustered by the unnerv-ingly prompt way her imagination suggested a different and frankly much more interesting fantasy that involved Max, the hands cradling his cup and nakedness on the kitchen table, Flora willed the colour in her cheeks to fade. 'My *culinary* fantasy,' she amended, her gaze sliding away.

'Ah.'

There was a silence. Curses, now she couldn't get that fantasy out of her head. And with Max Kennard, of all people! If she was going to fantasize, Flora wanted it to be about someone sexy and fun; not a man who couldn't be bothered to smile properly and had nothing to recommend him except a cool, firm mouth, and capable-looking hands, and what looked as if it would be a solid body, and . . . what exactly was her problem with that fantasy again?

Good grief, she had to pull herself together. Flora cleared her throat, and made a big deal of searching for some frangipane tarts she had made the day before. The bulk of them were destined for a café in Ayesborough, but she had put aside a few to break the ice with Max.

Although, frankly, grappling each other naked on the table would be a much better way of warming things up.

Stop it, Flora told herself, horrified by the way her wayward brain had grabbed on to that stupid fantasy and was busily galloping away with it. This was Sir Max Kennard, village squire and Hope's brother and out of her league on absolutely every count. Quite apart from being very poor fantasy material. Really, why not pick someone incredibly handsome to fantasize about? And not just handsome. If she was going to have a fantasy, she should make it a good one — about a prince like Hope's, perhaps; or some billionaire businessman relocating to Combe St Philip for some unspecified reason (it was just a fantasy, after all).

She had to spend the next few

months with Max. Fantasizing about him was totally inappropriate, not to mention pointless.

She was absolutely not going to do it.

2

It was time to get businesslike. 'Have a frangipane tart,' Flora offered, hoping that some sugar might sweeten his mood. She pushed the tin across the table towards Max. 'What time will the kitchen be free in the mornings?' she asked as he peered in the tin and took one of the dainty confections.

'I'm usually out and about by seven.' Max took a bite of the tartlet and chewed, raising his brows in a gesture of approval. 'Good,' he commented, and Flora was absurdly pleased by his praise.

She was less delighted to see him take another tartlet, break it apart, and toss half each to the two dogs who had finished shredding newspaper and, scenting treats, were now sitting by his chair looking alert. One was a shaggy thing with a dopey expression, the other a bristly terrier. They caught the pieces of tart in the air with a snap of their jaws and gulped them down. Flora thought of the exquisitely delicate pastry she had made, the filling of just the right consistency and the almond flavour perfectly balanced, and sighed.

Max was outlining his morning. He had converted one of outbuildings to a studio from which he ran his landscape design business, but first thing every morning he walked the dogs to the great glasshouses beyond the kitchen garden where he ran what Hope said was a surprisingly profitable sideline producing pot plants for hotels and offices.

'I'll give you a key so that you can let yourself in and out the back door,' Max said now. 'You can park by the stables, which will be more convenient than trekking through the great hall every day.'

'I think I'll walk most days,' said Flora, nobly ignoring the temptation to comment on how thoroughly she had been reduced to servant status. 'It's a lovely walk up from the village. I'm anxious not to get in your way, though.'

'You won't bother me,' he said brusquely. 'I might come in to make the occasional coffee or slap a sandwich together, but that's all I use the kitchen for.'

'I can tell.' Flora tried not to shudder at the idea of slapping a sandwich together. She wouldn't be able to watch. 'You don't have what I'd call a well-equipped kitchen.'

'I've got everything I need,' he pointed out.

'That would be the can opener?'

Max eyed her severely. 'I don't like a lot of fuss about food — or about anything, in fact.'

'Mm. You might have to change your attitude before June. If there's one thing a wedding means, it's fuss; and when it comes to a royal wedding, it'll be fuss multiplied to power of ten.'

'Tell me about it,' sighed Max, thinking of the refurbishments he was already planning. The décor in the manor was very tired, and he would have to redecorate at the very least before Hope's big day. She was planning a marquee in the garden for the reception, but guests would be in and out of the manor itself all day in search of bathrooms and somewhere to leave their coats or freshen their lipstick or whatever else women did when they disappeared at functions.

Apparently the Crown Prince and Princess of San Michele could not be expected to use the same loo as everyone else, and he would need to install a brand-new one reserved for their sole use on the day. What about all the other princes and princesses who would be there? Would they expect their own facilities too? And then there would be bridesmaids staying the night before . . .

Max's head started to spin whenever he thought about everything that was involved in this supposedly simple wedding. He didn't mind the house being shabby, but he didn't want Hope to feel ashamed of it; and if the royals in San Michele were being sniffy about the wedding being here, the least he could do for his sister was make sure everything was looking its best on her wedding day.

'It's exciting, though, isn't it?' Flora smiled encouragingly at him.

'If you like that sort of thing.'

'You mean, like glamour and romance? Royalty, champagne, incredible frocks, handsome men, sparkling jewels? Oh, wait, you're right, that's just dull, dull, dull.'

Max was disconcerted by her teasing. Most people were too intimidated by his frown or impressed by his title but Flora seemed to think that he was amusing. He couldn't decide if he liked it or not.

'It's all very well to get excited about a wedding,' he said austerely, 'but we don't know much about this Jonas yet, do we? I mean, he's a prince — fine — but what kind of man is he?' He frowned at Flora. 'You're her friend. You women talk about these things. What do *you* think about him?'

'I think Hope loves him, and that's what's important.'

'But what's he *like*?'

'I don't know him any better than you do, but he must be pretty special to have got her to agree to marry him at all, don't you think?'

'That's true.' Max brooded a moment, absently tugging on Bella's ears. 'I just want her to be happy,' he found himself confessing. 'She's had a tough time.'

Flora's expression softened. 'I know,' she said. 'But Hope has always known her own mind, and I think she's marrying Jonas in spite of the fact that he's a prince, not because of it.'

Max hoped she was right. He'd only met Jonas briefly, and it hadn't been long enough to really get the measure of him.

'I'm just concerned that they're rushing into things,' he said. 'Once you start talking weddings, everything snowballs, and before you know where you are, it's out of control and you can't stop it.'

Flora had been drinking her coffee, but now she put her cup back in its saucer, and studied him with those bright blue eyes. 'Is that what happened when you got married?' she asked nosily.

How had he got into this conversation? Max wondered. He *never* talked about personal matters. Flora might live in the same village, but to all intents and purposes she was a stranger. It was just that when she sat there looking at him with her head slightly tilted and her expression warm and interested, he felt strangely compelled to tell her.

'A bit. Yes, it was. Not that I didn't want to marry Stella,' he added hastily. 'I did. She was — is — beautiful, but we were both very young. I was only twenty-three, and I — '

He stopped. He'd been about to tell Flora Deare of all people that he'd been desperate to believe that somebody loved him. He'd fallen hard for Stella when he met her at university. Max could still see her as she'd been then, with her cloud of dark hair and great pansy eyes, so fragile-looking and sweet. He had hardly been able to believe that she would love him back, so when she started talking about marriage, of course he'd agreed.

He'd assumed that they would be married in a few years' time, but Stella had been thrilled, and suddenly it was announcements and engagement parties and fevered discussions about dates and dresses and he'd wanted time to breathe, to suggest that they stopped for a while and thought about what they were doing. But Stella had been happy, and he hadn't known how to put on the brakes until it was far too late.

Flora was waiting for him to finish. *I was young*, he intended to say, but instead when he opened his mouth, something else entirely came out. 'I was afraid of losing her,' he said.

'I'm not surprised,' she said. 'She's very beautiful.'

'You know Stella?'

'Hope showed me your wedding photos. I think she was trying to cure me.'

'Cure you?'

'Of my broken heart,' she explained kindly.

Max stared at her. 'What?'

'Yep.' Flora nodded. 'I had a *massive* crush on you when I was fifteen. Oh, don't look so appalled,' she added with a mischievous glint. 'I'm over you now, of course, but at the time . . . wow, that hurt! I mean, what were you thinking, preferring to marry a gorgeous, slim, charming woman your own age instead of waiting for a fat, awkward adolescent to grow up?'

'Foolish of me,' he said with a sardonic look, and Flora was pleased to see that oddly lost expression as he recalled his marriage vanish into his more customary dourness.

She hadn't made the crush up. She hadn't known Hope in those days, and Max was a distant figure. On the rare occasions he came into the shop, he seemed guarded and aloof, but that had only added to his mystique. He was Max Kennard, after all, heir to the baronetcy and beautiful Hasebury Hall.

That had been before the big scandal, when Gerald Kennard and his socialite wife, Georgie, had brought glamour to quiet Combe St Philip, running through the fortune built up by generations of more prudent Kennards.

Max and Hope were packed off to boarding school so that Georgie and Gerald could ski in Gstaad or Aspen in the winter. They spent their summers on yachts in the Caribbean or in villas overlooking the Mediterranean. There was a flat in New York and a house in London. On the rare occasions that they were at home in Combe St Philip, they threw lavish house parties. Celebrity guests roared through the village in their sports cars and took over the pub with their careless, golden arrogance. Sometimes they came into her grandparents' shop and bought up vast quantities of gin or cigarettes. It was all enormously exciting and livened up the village, which was torn between disapproval and pride.

Max was the opposite of his flamboyant father. As a girl, Flora had found his reserve intriguing, but studying him now across the kitchen table, she wondered how hard it had been to be so obviously out of place in his parents' jet-set lifestyle.

Max took another tart and inspected it closely, while the dogs quivered in anticipation. 'How do you get them so perfect?' he asked.

'Practice,' said Flora, tacitly accepting the change of subject. 'I spent two years at Mezzaluna as a pastry chef under Paolo Sparchetti, and I could make them in my sleep by the time I left.'

Even Max had heard of Mezzaluna and Paolo Sparchetti, the famously temperamental chef whose restaurant was showered with accolades and Michelin stars. Personally, he had better things to spend his money on — even without the need to install a new lavatory for royalty — but Flora must be good if she had worked there.

'Hope said you were thinking of opening your own restaurant in London,' he said, and she sighed a little as she pushed her empty coffee cup away.

'That was the plan. I was going to go into partnership with my boyfriend, who's also a chef, but *brilliant*, and we were starting to look at properties, but then . . . well, Pops was struggling without Granny, and I was worried about him. He was getting more and more confused, so I moved back here to keep an eye on him.'

'Couldn't your mother have looked after him?'

Flora pulled a face. 'She's been in an ashram in India for the last couple of years. It's not that she doesn't care, it's just . . . well, she's not very practical.'

That was putting it mildly, thought Max. In her own way, Flora's mother was as notorious in Combe St Philip as his father had been. Christened, sensibly, Sarah, she had run off to join a cult at eighteen and changed her name to Sky. Periodically, she would return to see her parents, wearing weird and wonderful robes that made the villagers stare, and spouting what was generally agreed to be nonsense about whatever religion or cult she happened to be following at the time.

When Hope had had to face down the pointing fingers and the humiliation of being the odd one out, Flora had understood, and they had been friends ever since.

'I'm sorry about your grandfather,' Max said in a rough voice. He remembered finding Norman Deare wandering around the manor gardens in his pyjamas one day. They'd had a long conversation about staking dahlias before Max had been able to guide him home. 'He was a good man.'

Flora's expression softened. 'Yes, he was special. Granny, too. I miss them both.'

'I suppose the cottage is yours now?'

She nodded. 'Yes.'

Norman Deare had died in the summer, nearly five months ago. The whole village had turned out for his funeral. It was the only time Max had seen Flora in black, and her face had been white and strained, but she had still greeted everyone with a smile — and the wake, he had heard, had been legendary.

'I thought you'd have gone back to London by now.' Max glanced around at the clutter Flora had brought into his kitchen, all in the name of her catering business. 'I don't understand why you're spending your time making cakes here when it sounds like you're much more interested in running a fancy restaurant.'

'I am, but unfortunately, the fancy restaurant option fell through with my relationship.' Flora's smile was a little too bright to be convincing. 'Rich — my boyfriend — wasn't exactly supportive about me coming back to look after Pops. He was furious that I was going just when we were ready to set up a place of our own, and I do see that it was frustrating for him; but he gave me an ultimatum, and there wasn't a choice as far as I was concerned. Pops had to come first.'

'It must have been tough for you,' Max said.

'Well, I've had better years,' she acknowledged, 'but I'll just have to set up my own restaurant. That's been my dream since I was eight.'

'Eight? That's early to be dreaming about restaurants, isn't it?'

'My grandparents took me out for lunch for my birthday that year. It wasn't long after I came to live with them, and I'd never experienced anything like it.' She smiled at the memory. 'It was just an ordinary café, really, but I thought it was wonderful. Everything was pretty and people were enjoying themselves. I felt so grown-up to be choosing from a menu, and when the food came, I thought it was the most delicious thing I had ever tasted. I swore there and then I'd have a restaurant of my own one day.

'And I still will,' she said, putting up her chin. 'It would have been nice to have done it with Rich, but I don't need him. I just need to sell the cottage and then move on to the next stage. It'll need a bit of money to set up because I want to be in London. I'm a city girl now, and for a cutting-edge restaurant, that's really the only place to be, but you know what London prices are like. I'll need investors.'

Good luck with that, thought Max, remembering his own financial woes. In his experience, investors were never around when you needed them. But there was no point in bursting Flora's bubble.

'It's very good of you to stay until Hope's wedding in that case,' he said.

'Oh, I'm not staying because of the wedding — of course I would always have come back to do that.'

Max was surprised. 'Then why are

you still here? Are you having problems with probate?'

'No, nothing like that. I can't sell the cottage yet.'

'Why not?'

'You wouldn't understand.'

'Try me.'

'Because of Sweetie,' Flora admitted.

There was a pause. 'Sweetie?' he echoed tonelessly.

'My grandparents' cat. It's an awful name, isn't it? And totally inappropriate, I've never met a cat who was *less* sweet, but they adored him. Anyway, Sweetie's very elderly now, and Pops was really worried about what would happen to him. I promised that I'd look after him. He's too old to adjust to a new home or a new owner; so as long as he's alive, he gets to stay in the cottage, and I have to stay with him. I said you wouldn't understand,' she finished accusingly, obviously reading Max's expression without difficulty.

'Dear God,' he said. 'You're putting your life on hold for a *cat*?'

'I promised,' she said simply. 'And don't tell me you wouldn't do same for those dogs,' she added, nodding down at Bella, who had abandoned hope of another frangipane tart and was lying in a shaggy heap on the floor, and Ted, still keeping an alert eye on Max.

'Dogs are different,' said Max firmly. 'Cats don't care about anyone but themselves.'

'It's true that Sweetie isn't the cuddliest of cats,' Flora admitted. 'But he's very beautiful.'

'Dogs have beautiful souls,' said Max. 'Take Bella,' he said. 'She was neglected as a puppy and when I took her, her coat was matted and dirty. Look at her now!'

Flora looked. 'I can tell she's got quite a varied ancestry,' she said tactfully.

'She's mostly bearded collie, I reckon, but with some Labrador and something else.' Probably something brainless. Much as Max loved Bella, even he had to admit that she was stupid. Still, every time she stood still to let him brush her, his throat thickened at her willingness to trust him.

'What about the other one?'

'That's Ted. I was walking along the lane over the bridge one day when I saw a van slow down and throw something out onto the riverbank. When I got there, I saw it was Ted.' Max reached down to stroke Ted's bristly head. 'The poor chap broke his leg, and he still walks with a limp, don't you? He was badly bruised and cut up.'

'Poor thing,' said Flora. 'It was good of you to take him home.'

'I knew how he felt. That was the day Stella left me. I was feeling a bit battered and bruised myself.'

And where had *that* come from? Max wondered. He scowled.

'Anyway, they've both given back more in loyalty and trust and affection than a cat ever could,' he said.

Flora pointed at him. 'You're a big softie under that grim lord-of-the-manor act!'

She was smiling, her eyes very blue.

She wasn't beautiful, Max reminded himself, or even particularly pretty. Her features were very ordinary, but she had lovely creamy skin and a temptingly lush figure. She looked soft . . . and warm . . . and . . . what were they talking about?

With an effort, Max pulled his mind back on track. For a moment there he had felt quite dizzy. He cleared his throat.

'Says the woman who's not selling her cottage because of a cat called Sweetie!'

Flora held up her hands to acknowledge the hit. 'I was bitten by a farm collie when I was six,' she said, 'and I've been nervous of dogs ever since. I mean, I like them in principle, but they always seem to have very big teeth.'

'Well, I can promise Bella and Ted won't bite you. We'll have to agree to disagree on cats and dogs.'

'I'm sure that's not all we'll disagree on,' said Flora gaily. 'Real coffee versus instant, cooking versus opening a can, city versus country . . . oh, and I'm cheery and you're cranky.'

'Good to know that we're not made for each other,' said Max, with a sarcastic look, but when Flora just laughed in agreement, he couldn't help feeling just a little bit . . . well, cranky.

3

Humming to herself, Flora drizzled lime juice and sugar carefully over a row of coconut cakes. A wet day had meant the lights had been on since the morning, and outside a blustery wind hurled rain at the windows, but inside it was warm and cosy with the combined heat of the range and the oven that had been going all day. She was enjoying the tranquillity of a kitchen on a winter afternoon, so different from the frenetic activity of a restaurant. Flora felt a little guilty about not missing that part of her life more, but now that she had unpacked everything, the kitchen was starting to feel like hers.

She had been making patisserie for a café in Ayesborough: chocolate and salted caramel tarts, delicately green pistachio slices, tiny apple tarte tatins, and individual strawberry cakes topped with jelly and garnished with white chocolate, strawberries and edible pearls. The café had requested some traditional cakes, too, so Flora had produced a couple of chocolate cakes, some coffee and walnut, a big Victoria sponge, and a selection of drizzle cakes. Once she would have turned her nose up at such plain baking and relished the challenge of making food innovative and exciting instead, but she had to admit that there had been something soothing about the simple tasks of measuring out butter and sugar, of cracking eggs into a bowl and sifting flour.

She would get back to real cooking once she was in London again, Flora reassured herself. She was more than just a pastry chef and she didn't want to lose her edge.

In the meantime, she might as well make the most of this. There was no competition in Combe St Philip, no challenge, no driving desire for perfection. There was just Sweetie to care for, and Hope's wedding to plan, and cakes to bake in this lovely kitchen.

Flora loved to think about the other cooks who had worked at the great scrubbed table. She had set her best dishes on the dresser, and hung her gleaming saucepans from the old hooks by the range. The fridge was defrosted and properly stocked, Max's meagre supplies banished to a lower shelf. In the larder, bowls of eggs sat on the marble shelf, and flour, sugar, nuts, spices and all the other dry ingredients she needed were arrayed in carefully labelled containers. Her cookbooks were stashed on a shelf near the tatty old chair by the range, and she had a notebook open on the table so that she could jot down any ideas for tweaks to recipes.

She had dragged in a sagging armchair from the old housekeeper's room, and her morning ritual was already established: a coffee and few minutes curled up in the chair with her feet tucked beneath her. It was her time to think about what she would cook for Hope's wedding. She would leaf through the books, and scribble notes . . . and, yes, all right, sometimes her mind *would* drift a little and she would imagine having a kitchen like this of her own, with a vegetable garden right outside the door. It would be lovely in summer, with the kitchen door open and sunlight puddling on the worn flagstones and the scent of an English summer garden heady on the air. She would have a jar of daisies on the windowsill and herbs handy in a stone trough just outside the door.

'Good to see you're working hard.'

Of course, Max had to choose to come in the moment she had sat down. She had seen little of him since the day he had helped carry in her equipment. He tended to use the side door into the boot room, which smelt of dogs and leather and old coats, and would grunt a greeting when he passed the kitchen door, but that morning he had come inside while she was dreaming. He'd obviously taken off his muddy boots, and was padding around in thick socks as the dogs bustled in behind him.

He had been working outside and his face was ruddy with cold. His hair was spangled with damp and his lashes clumped in the wet, accentuating the keen green of his eyes. He wore old trousers and a blue jumper with a hole that was unravelling at the elbow. His face was set in its usual irascible expression.

So there was absolutely no reason for Flora's pulse to kick up a notch.

'I *am* working, as it happens,' she said. 'I'm planning the canapés for Hope's wedding.' She scowled at Bella who had shambled over to thrust her hairy nose into Flora's lap. Flora pushed her away — but carefully. Max could say what he liked about Bella being soft, but she still had big teeth.

Glancing up, she caught the glint of amusement in his eyes, and her treacherous pulse kicked up a little further.

'Can't you teach those dogs of yours to wipe their feet when they come in?' she demanded, hoping that he couldn't see the warmth that burned in her cheeks. 'Look at the mess they've made of my nice clean floor!'

'I hate to remind you, Flora, but it's actually my floor,' Max pointed out, though he grabbed some kitchen paper and wiped up most of the mess.

'Want some coffee?' she asked, mollified, as she uncurled herself from the chair.

'Is it going to take half a day to make?'

Flora tsked. 'It's easy.' She reached into the freezer for the coffee beans, and ground them quickly. 'Here, let me show you so that you can help yourself if I'm not here,' she said. 'Fill the water, like this . . . '

After a moment, Max moved nearer and stood beside her to watch. Which was exactly what she had invited. Only now he seemed larger and more solid, and she was distracted, fumbling with the portafilter, suddenly all thumbs.

'So, um, you dose the coffee in here — see.'

47

'What does 'dose' mean?' He leant closer and Flora's mind promptly went blank.

What *did* it mean? He smelt good, of rain and the clean smell of outdoors, and although he wasn't touching her — nowhere near — she could *feel* the warmth radiating from him, like a glow down her side.

Unless she was the one who was warm? It was hard to tell.

He was waiting for her to answer. What had been the question again? Oh, yes, dose. Desperately, she cleared her throat.

'Er, it's just about measuring in the coffee.' Hallelujah, more than two words strung together in a coherent order.

Max wasn't much taller than she was, but there was something rock-like about him. If you leant against him, he wouldn't fall over — and he wouldn't disappear like Rich, whose lack of support still stung, for all she told everyone that it had all been for the best.

Flora wrenched her wayward thoughts

back into line. 'So, yes, you dose the coffee and tamp it down in the puck, like so.' She demonstrated. 'Then you just switch *this* . . . and *this* . . . and voilà! Perfect coffee. Want to have a go?'

Max hesitated, and she looked at him more closely. 'You didn't listen to a word I said, did you?'

He had the grace to look uncomfortable. 'I've got a lot on my mind.'

She relented. 'Here, you'd better take this one.'

He took the mug with a grunt of thanks. 'I don't know why you can't just boil a kettle and pour it over some granules,' he grumbled, but she noticed that he was drinking it without complaint.

It was a relief that he had moved away. Flora concentrated hard on making her own coffee, and on not noticing how oddly right he looked leaning casually against the kitchen counter.

'It looks a bit different in here now,' said Max, glancing around him as if visualizing all the boxes and bags which had filled the room that Monday morning.

'I told you I would clear it all away,' Flora pointed out. 'I put all the boxes in one of the empty rooms down the passage. I'll need them all again when I move out at the end of June.'

Already the thought was depressing.

'It's a lovely kitchen to work in,' she told him, following his gaze. The high ceilings, the light through the big windows and all that wonderful work space . . . knowing that she could open a cupboard and there would be just the utensil she wanted.

'Ah yes, this is you living your fantasy,' Max remembered.

'You can mock,' said Flora with dignity, 'but at least I'm living mine. How many people can say that?'

'Not me, that's for sure.'

'I'd love to ask you what your fantasy would be, but that would probably be asking for trouble.'

'It would,' said Max. 'I prefer to keep

my fantasies private.'

'Ooh, now I *really* want to know what they are!'

Max put down his coffee. He wished she wouldn't smile at him like that. It made him . . . twitchy. He wasn't the kind of man who flirted or had fun. He didn't want to be amused or grin back at her. Especially, he didn't want to think about fantasies and Flora in the same breath.

He scowled instead. 'How is your sitting tenant?' he asked, unable to bring himself to ask directly after an animal called Sweetie. Surely they could have found a decent name for the cat?

'In fine form,' said Flora cheerfully. 'He bites my ankles if I don't feed him the moment I get in. Look.' She pulled up her jeans a little way to show him a selection of scratches and tooth marks.'

'Those look painful.' Max cleared his throat. Please God he wasn't really aroused by the glimpse of an ankle, like some dirty Victorian! He might as well grow a pair of mutton-chop whiskers and be done with it.

He had kept away from the kitchen as much as possible over the last couple of days, but he'd been very aware of Flora all the same. He'd heard her humming happily to herself when he passed the door, and delicious smells drifted out to the boot room.

He'd let himself be lured in today by the scent of coffee and freshly made cake, but now he wished he hadn't. He'd meant to get a coffee, tell her about the kids and go, but instead she had beckoned him over to the coffee machine, and like a fool he had gone to stand next to her. He'd been excruciatingly aware of her. Strands of gold in the choppy blonde hair glinted in the overhead light and he could smell her shampoo, something fresh and sweet, like the garden on a summer morning.

How hard could it be to make coffee? Max had tried to concentrate on what she was telling him, but kept getting distracted by how the tinge of pink along her cheekbones warmed the creamy skin. She had beautiful hands with short, very clean nails, and he would find his gaze fixated on her pointing finger without taking in anything that she was saying. And then she had glanced at him and accused him of not listening, blue eyes brimming with amusement, and Max had felt something unlock inside him.

'I wouldn't put up with that if I were you,' he said sternly, eyes almost crossing in the effort of not smiling back at her.

'Oh, he doesn't mean it. He's just old and missing Pops. He's allowed to be cranky.'

Unlike you. She didn't say it, but Max could practically see the words hovering on her tongue.

'I really just came in to remind you that Holly and Ben will be here tonight.' Max assumed his most forbidding expression, though it didn't have much effect on Flora.

'I haven't forgotten. I thought I'd

make macaroni cheese. Most children like that. Will that be okay for Holly and Ben?'

'I should think they'd be delighted with anything that wasn't spaghetti bolognaise, which is all that I can cook,' said Max.

'Excellent. I'll find out what they do and don't like later.'

'Stella's going to drop them off after school. I daresay she'll come in and check you out.'

'You haven't told her about my crush and how I hated her for marrying you?'

'Why on earth would I have told her that?' said Max irritably.

'I would have,' Flora said.

'Well, I can assure you that I haven't discussed you at all with Stella, other than to say that you're using the kitchen and that I've arranged for you to give the kids a decent meal at least once a week.'

Flora knew that Hope loathed Stella. 'She hurt Max,' she'd said flatly. 'Max always pretends that it was all for the best, but I know that he was gutted at the time.' So while Flora was intrigued to meet Max's ex-wife, she wasn't predisposed to like her.

Still, when Stella arrived with the two children later as she was drizzling sugar syrup onto the cakes, Flora had to admit that she was super friendly.

Stella was tiny and fragile-looking with huge eyes and glossy dark hair. Flora felt enormous next to her. No wonder Max was so morose, knowing that he'd lost someone quite so beautiful. It must be so hard for him to see Stella, Flora realized. His ex was stunning still, and beautifully dressed, and apparently sweet-natured.

A nightmare, in fact.

Ben's eyes rounded when he saw the spread of cakes on the great table. 'Can we have one?' he asked.

'Ben!' Stella rolled her beautiful eyes. 'Flora, I'm so sorry! You must think I've brought along a couple of savages!'

'It's fine,' said Flora, who liked the way Ben had cut to the chase. He looked like a nice boy, a typically scruffy nine-year-old, with his shirt half-in and half-out of his trousers and his hair standing on end. Had Max looked like this when he was a little boy? Flora suspected not. He looked as if he had sprung fully grown from the womb with a disapproving expression. 'Of course you can,' she told Ben. 'You can have a chocolate or a Victoria sponge.'

There followed a brief tussle between the two children, until they settled on chocolate.

'That's what I wanted him to choose anyway,' said Holly loftily. 'I only chose the Victoria sponge because I knew he'd go for the chocolate to spite me.'

According to Hope, who adored her, Holly was ten-and-a-half going on twenty-five. Holly looked like Hope too, with a tumble of coppery curls and an enchantingly pretty face saved from cuteness by the sharp expression in her green eyes.

With a mental apology to Hope,

Flora felt obliged to offer Stella a cup of tea. She would have liked to have showed off her coffee maker, but it was after four o'clock, and this was England, after all. Tea it had to be.

Stella accepted tea but, unlike her children, refused a slice of cake. 'Christmas is coming up,' she explained, patting her perfectly flat stomach. 'You know how one piles on the pounds at this time of year!'

Flora did know, and had the figure to prove it. She doubted if Stella had ever overindulged in her life, though. A second lettuce leaf would be Stella's idea of going too far. There was no way she could stay so slender otherwise.

Defiantly, Flora poured tea and helped herself to cake while Stella settled down for a cosy chat.

'We're all so excited about Hope marrying a prince! What a relief to be able to talk to you about it, though,' Stella said. 'It's been so hard keeping it a secret!'

'I know. I ring Ally up every now and

then, and we have a little squeal: *Omigod, Hope's going to be a princess!'*

'I'm going to be a bridesmaid,' Holly announced importantly.

'Hey, me too!' They regarded each other with pleasure.

'*Really?*' Stella sipped at her tea and studied her over the rim of her cup. Flora could practically hear her calculating that she must be twice the size of Hope. 'I didn't realize you and Hope were that close.'

'We've been friends for a long time. My first cooking job was at the Three Bells, and I got to know Hope when she got a weekend job there.'

'Oh, yes, that *ghastly* time.' Stella sighed. 'I don't know why Hope insisted on getting that job. She was only fifteen. Max made sure she had everything she needed.'

Except a father, thought Flora.

Holly wasn't interested in old family scandals. 'Hope says we can go to London to choose our bridesmaid dresses,' she told Flora. 'She says there's a shop where if you're a VIP you can go in the back door, and you have a whole room to yourself and a personal shopper brings you stuff to try on while you drink champagne.'

'That sounds like fun,' Flora agreed. 'I'm up for that. As long as Hope doesn't want to put us in anything frilly.'

She was joking, but Stella took her seriously. 'Frills would be a mistake for you, Flora,' she said. 'You're quite . . . tall, aren't you?'

'I'm going to look ridiculous next to Hope and Ally and Holly,' Flora agreed cheerfully, with a wink at Holly. 'I'm hoping they'll airbrush me out of all the photos. What about you, Ben?' she asked. 'Are you going to be a pageboy?'

He pulled a face. 'No way!'

'I wish you would, Ben,' said Stella fretfully. 'I'm sure Prince Jonas's nephews will be in the bridal party.'

'I'm not getting dressed up.' Ben's face set in a stubborn expression that made him look remarkably like his father. 'Hope said I didn't need to if I didn't want to, and I don't. Holly can wear a stupid dress if she wants.'

Luckily the two dogs bustled into the kitchen just then and put a stop to a fiery argument between the two children. The dogs were followed by Max, and for an odd moment, Flora's pulse leapt, as if she had missed a step in the dark and had only just righted herself in time.

'Dad!' Holly scrambled from her chair and threw herself at him, talking a mile a minute about some party she had been invited to. Max's smile as he bent over his daughter gave Flora a jolt. He was only thirty-six, but he was so dour that he usually looked older than that. Now, though, ruffling Ben's hair, he seemed younger, and really . . . well, really quite attractive. He'd been working in his studio and was still wearing his glasses, stern horn-rimmed affairs that should have looked ridiculous but actually made him seem pretty cool.

Stella rose gracefully from the table and wafted towards him, lifting her cheek for a kiss. 'Hello, darling,' she said. 'It's so lovely that Flora knows about Hope's engagement. It means we can talk about it with someone at last.'

'Great. As long as *I* don't have to talk about it.' Max's gaze met Flora's briefly. 'I see you've met Holly and Ben?'

'Yes, we've been bonding over bridesmaids' dresses,' Flora managed. Her voice sounded alarmingly thin, as if her lungs had been squeezed of air.

'Max,' Stella interrupted. 'Did you get my email about Christmas? There's so much going on, it's an absolute nightmare. Ben's class has got a Christmas fair, and there's Holly's dance event, and then the carol concert . . . You don't want to miss any of them, do you?'

'God forbid,' said Max straight-faced and Stella made a show of rolling her eyes at him.

'They'd both be devastated if you

61

weren't there, you know.'

He sighed. 'I'll be there, Stella.'

'And we'll see you for Christmas lunch as usual? It means so much to Holly and Ben that you're there too,' Stella went on. 'I couldn't bear for you to be here on your own . . . unless you've got other plans?' she asked artlessly.

There was a tiny pause. 'No, no other plans,' said Max.

'Tell me, how did you get on with Cressida?'

'Fine,' said Max, doing a good impression of a stag at bay.

Stella clapped her hands. 'I *thought* you'd get on! She's lovely, isn't she?'

'Yes, she's very nice.'

Mr Chatty. Flora, who had gone back to her icing, rolled her eyes inwardly. You'd think Stella would have known better than to try and get an enthusiastic response out of Max.

'Are you going to see her again?'

Max's eyes flickered to Flora and then away. 'We're having dinner tomorrow,' he conceded reluctantly.

'Ooh, exciting!'

'It's just dinner, Stella,' he said, ignoring her moue of disappointment. 'I've got enough to do getting the house ready for Hope's wedding. A relationship is the last thing I need at the moment.'

★ ★ ★

The children had drifted away and Flora was grating cheese by the time Max finally saw Stella off and went back to the kitchen. Bella and Ted were sitting by her, looking alert in the hope of a dropped scrap or two, while Flora seemed to be doing her best to ignore them.

'Do you always let them beg like this?' she asked Max disapprovingly.

'They like cheese.' It seemed a good enough explanation to Max.

'Still, it's a bit degrading. Look at them, all big eyes and drooling and hopeful expressions,' she said with a disparaging glance downwards at the two dogs. 'You'd never get Sweetie carrying on like that. He just expects his treats served up on a gold plate without him even having to ask for them.'

'That's cats for you,' said Max, stealing a couple of pieces of cheese and tossing them to Bella and Max, who gulped eagerly at them. 'Dogs are much more appreciative.'

Flora sniffed, evidently unconvinced. She shook the last gratings of cheese into a bowl and set a pan on the hob with a knob of butter.

'Does your ex-wife organize all your dates for you?'

'They're not exactly *dates*,' said Max, hunching a shoulder. 'It's just going out for a drink or dinner.'

'That sounds awfully like a date to me.'

'It's awkward,' he admitted grudgingly. 'Stella keeps introducing me to these friends of hers and they're obviously expecting me to ask them out, and frankly it's easier to invite them for a drink than try and think of some excuse.'

Flora raised her brows. 'You don't strike me as the kind of man who does anything he doesn't want to do. Why don't you tell Stella to stop fixing you up?'

'I've tried telling her that I'm perfectly happy on my own, but she's got this idea that Holly and Ben need me to give them an example of a 'loving relationship'.' He hooked his fingers in the air as if his tone hadn't already told Flora all she needed to know what he thought about it. 'I've pointed out that she and Marcus are already providing a good example, but Stella thinks I should do the same, and she manages to imply that by not doing that, I'm letting Holly and Ben down somehow. My ex-wife has emotional blackmail down to a fine art,' he added as he pinched a piece of cheese for himself.

Flora pulled a sympathetic face. 'That's tough. I know what it's like, though. I had a boyfriend once whose ex was the queen of emotional black-mail. Sam told me about her soon after we got together. He said that even though she'd met someone else, they had ended things amicably and decided to stay friends. Which I thought was fine. Very civilized. Who could possibly object to that?

'When I met Michelle, she was very friendly. I thought she was nice, in fact, but then I realized that she was ringing Sam whenever anything went wrong. She needed a lift home, or she'd lost her keys, or the tap was dripping, or her new boyfriend had made her cry . . . ' Flora sighed and shook her head at the memory of it. 'Sam said I didn't understand. Michelle had had a bad time, he said. She was very vulnerable. They were friends; how could he refuse to help her? And so on and so forth.'

She peered into her pan, shaking it on the element. 'I thought Michelle was just jerking his chain. She didn't want Sam as a boyfriend but she didn't want him to move on either, for all she was so friendly. Sam was supposed to be pining for *her*, not having fun with someone new. But of course Sam didn't want to hear what I thought. I suppose she was right and that he wasn't ready for a new relationship. I gave up in the end,' Flora told Max. 'It was sad. I really liked Sam, but I soon got tired of waiting for him to decide which girlfriend he really wanted.'

'Stella's not like that,' said Max, frowning uneasily.

'That's good,' said Flora. 'I wouldn't wish that situation on anyone. And I can see it's hard. You've got children together. It's not as if you can cut Stella out of your life.'

'Exactly,' said Max. For a minute there he had thought Flora might not understand. And it was only afterwards that he asked himself why he cared whether she did or not.

4

When Flora walked into the Three Bells that night, Ally was already perched at the bar. She had shooed away a couple of men who were lurking hopefully, and patted the stool beside her. Unwinding her scarf, Flora climbed onto it, pink-faced and glowing from the cold. She was wearing a lime-green top and felt like the Jolly Green Giant next to Ally, who was slender and effortlessly stylish, with sparkling hazel eyes and glossy brown hair that she had twisted up and secured casually.

'I hate the way you do that thing with your hair,' Flora said by way of greeting. 'Like you haven't even thought about it but it still looks perfect.'

'I *haven't* thought about it,' Ally pointed out. 'I hope you've got a good excuse for being late, Floradear?'

Flora checked her phone. 18:32.

'Two minutes!' she protested.

'It feels like two hours with Jennifer glaring at me. I don't think she liked me hogging this stool for you.'

'Jennifer doesn't like anything.' Flora glanced across the bar to where Jennifer, the pinch-mouthed landlady of the Three Bells, was polishing glasses and assiduously ignoring all attempts to catch her eye. 'Have you ever wondered how someone who hates serving drinks comes to be running a pub?'

'Only every time I come in here,' said Ally.

'How do you think Pete stays married to her? He's so lovely and she's so . . . so . . . so *not*.' Pete Harmon had given Flora her very first job washing dishes in the kitchen. He was a big, jolly bear of a man, in complete contrast to his thin, sour wife. The nature of their marriage had long been a puzzle to Flora, Ally and Hope.

'Maybe it's like a fairy tale and Jennifer turns into a beautiful, sweet-natured princess at night?' Ally suggested.

Flora lowered her voice and glanced around to make sure no one could hear her. 'And talking of princesses . . . have you heard from Hope at all?'

'Not for a while, no. Why?'

'I just wanted to run some menu ideas past her.'

Ally regarded Flora with affection. 'I might have known you'd be thinking about the food already.'

'The trouble is that Hope wants simple, and I'd really like to show off,' she confessed.

'I'm sure you can squeeze some fancy twists in somewhere,' said Ally. 'Actually, I'd like to talk to Hope too. I've got an idea that I'd like to run past her.'

But Flora wasn't listening. Glancing idly at the pub door, she had seen a slim, very attractive woman come in. She was smiling and saying something over her shoulder to the dark, stern-looking man behind her.

Max.

The sight of him made Flora's heart jolt alarmingly, although she couldn't have said why. She had seen him briefly earlier that day, when he had grunted a reply to her cheery good morning. So there was no reason for every cell in her body to jump when he had walked into the pub.

It must be something to do with seeing him out of context, Flora realized. She was (sort of) used to him padding through the kitchen in socks and his old working clothes, but tonight he was dressed up, or as dressed up as one got for a drink in a country pub. He was wearing a pale yellow textured cotton shirt, open casually at the neck, and it suited him so well that Flora would have staked her life on the fact that Stella had bought it for him.

Over it, he wore an old tweed jacket with leather buttons. Very lord of the manor, Flora decided, trying to joke herself out of the ridiculously heightened sense of awareness. It wasn't even as if he were particularly handsome or charming. His expression was set in characteristically sardonic lines, overlaid with an aloofness that she had often seen when he was out in the village, but that was quite different from the way he looked at his children. For the first time it occurred to Flora that when your family name had been comprehensively dragged through the mud it might be easier to hide behind a mask of reserve.

She watched under her lashes as Max steered the woman — presumably Stella's friend Cressida — to a table.

'You're not listening to a word I'm saying, are you?' Ally dug Flora in the ribs with her elbow. 'Who are you looking at? Ohhhhh,' she added on a long-drawn-out note of interest before Flora could reply. She had already followed her gaze to the table across the room. 'Sir Max Kennard himself! Who's that with him?'

'Her name's Cressida, I think.'

'Cressida?' They exchanged a look and a little moue of agreement that the name wasn't for them, although Cressida's wardrobe met with more approval. Dark-haired and slender, she was elegantly dressed in narrow trousers, heels and the palest of pale pink cashmere jumpers with pearls at her throat and in her ears. Ally studied the outfit enviously. 'She's gorgeous, isn't she?'

Flora fingered the gaudy turquoise glass necklace at her own neck. 'I think the pearls are a bit boring, don't you?'

'Dullsville,' Ally agreed. 'Still, could we be looking at the next Lady Kennard? She's beautiful, glamorous, well-dressed . . . '

'Max said she was very nice, too,' Flora remembered glumly.

Ally flicked her a speculative glance. 'What's he like?'

'Max?' Flora looked at her in surprise. 'You must know, surely. You've known Hope much longer than I have.'

'I don't really know Max, though. He was always so much older than Hope. Either he was away at school or he'd left home. He always seemed as if he had a big stick up his bottom.'

'I know what you mean, but he's not so bad when you talk to him,' Flora said. 'He's never going to be Mr Charm, and he can be a bit cranky, but he's okay. He's been fine, actually. What?' she demanded when Ally just looked at her. 'He has!'

'Any resurrection of your little crush on him?'

'God, Ally, that was *years* ago! I should never have told you about it — and I wouldn't have if you hadn't poured a vat of gin down me,' Flora accused her friend.

'It was the night Rich the Rat dumped you. You needed it.'

'Anyway, I didn't really have a crush. I just . . . thought he seemed nice.'

You told me you cried for two whole days when you heard that he was going to marry Stella.'

'I was *fifteen*,' said Flora. 'Anyway, I was so over it a couple days later. I think I decided to be in love with someone a bit more attainable like Prince William instead.' She straightened a bar mat. 'Now you come to mention it, I seem to have a pattern of falling for unavailable men.'

Ally knew where that one was going. 'Rich wasn't unavailable,' she pointed out robustly. 'He was just incredibly selfish and self-centred.'

'I suppose.' Flora sighed a little and then gave herself a shake. She was the cheery one, not the kind of girl who moped about ex-boyfriends or felt depressed because Max was out on a date with a gorgeous, nice, glamorous woman. It was time to lift their mood.

'What do you think we have to do to get a drink from Jennifer?'

'I've tried waving to catch her attention, but she just ignores me,' said Ally. 'She hates me.'

'She hates me too,' Flora pointed out. 'It's weird, isn't it? I mean, who would hate us when we're so fantastic?'

'And charming.'

'And good fun.'

'Good company.'

'Perfectly behaved.'

'Except after a third gin.'

'Speak for yourself. I'm always

perfectly behaved.'

They were both laughing as Max approached the bar. He hesitated fractionally as he caught sight of them, but Flora wriggled her fingers at him in greeting and could practically see him realize that he wouldn't be able to ignore her.

'Flora.' Max nodded at her, and then at Ally. 'Ally.'

'Hi, Max.' Ally smiled at him.

'Sir Max!' Jennifer Harmon practically fell over herself to rush to Max's end of the bar.

She was a ghastly snob, and adored the Kennards, scandal or no scandal. Gerald Kennard's imprisonment had hit her almost as hard as it had the Kennards themselves, but she saw Max as the family's salvation. He might be short on glamour or his father's ebullient charm, but he had paid off all the debts and managed to hang on to the manor itself by the skin of his teeth, so there were still Kennards at Hasebury Hall. He could do no wrong in

Jennifer's eyes. Hope swore that she had once actually seen Jennifer curtsey, and Flora had never quite known whether she had been joking or not.

'How nice to see you in here!' she gushed, her smile sitting oddly on her normally sour face. 'What can I get you?'

'I think Flora and Ally are waiting to order,' Max said, tipping his head in their direction. 'They were here before me.'

Unable to refuse outright, Jennifer turned to them with a smile so acidulated that it was all Flora and Ally could do not to burst into giggles.

'Two large glasses of sauvignon blanc, please, Jennifer,' said Flora, 'and two packs of peanuts.'

'Thanks, Max,' said Ally, blowing him a kiss.

Jennifer plonked the two glasses in front of them, tossed the peanuts on the bar, and turned obsequiously back to Max, who ordered a small glass of chardonnay and a pint of bitter.

Flora lifted her glass and took a sip, momentarily distracted from Max as she narrowed her eyes and concentrated on the lovely zingy flavours: gooseberry and cut grass, a touch of lime perhaps, or was that grapefruit she could taste? She put down her glass while she savoured the effect on her taste buds.

'Say what you like about Jennifer,' she said to Ally, 'but she's introduced some decent wines. Remember what plonk they used to serve before she pushed Pete into turning the Three Bells into a gastropub?'

'I didn't know that was Jennifer's doing,' said Ally, distracted.

'You must remember what it was like! When I started helping in the kitchen we just churned out ordinary pub grub, but then they brought in Tom and got a proper wine buyer . . . Pete and Jennifer have transformed the Three Bells without losing the pub atmosphere.'

Ally pulled a face, unconvinced. 'The atmosphere is down to Pete. He's brilliant. If Jennifer had her way, she'd ban riff-raff like us and only serve titled people. Look at her with Max. It's revolting!'

'I know.' Flora leant closer to her friend. 'Imagine what she's going to be like when she hears that our best friend is going to be a princess,' she breathed in her ear so that no one could hear. 'She is so going to regret not being nicer to us,' she pronounced, and Ally had to clap a hand over her mouth to stop the snort of laughter.

'I've reserved a table in the restaurant for seven-thirty,' Max was telling Jennifer when Flora turned her attention back to him.

'Of course! I'll make sure it's ready for you.' Jennifer set the lovingly pulled beer and the glass of chardonnay carefully in front of him. 'I'll put all this on your tab, shall I?'

'Thank you.' Max looked relieved to escape.

Flora swivelled on her stool so that she could watch him carry the drinks back to the table, where Cressida smiled up at him, shaking back her glossy hair invitingly.

'Look at that! See how she's touching herself?' she said to Ally out of the corner of her mouth as Cressida fluttered her fingers along her beautiful clavicle. 'God, that's such a giveaway. And all that mirroring! Why not just throw herself across the table and beg him, 'Take me now!'?'

'Hmm.' Ally craned her neck to see round Flora. 'Doesn't look as if he's enjoying it much, though, does he?'

That was true. He didn't. Flora was ridiculously cheered to realize that Ally was right. Max's head was inclined courteously towards his companion, but his body language was definitely uncomfortable. Of course, that could be because she wasn't his Stella.

'Maybe you're in with a chance after all,' Ally suggested.

'Yeah, right. If I lost four stone and chopped six inches off my legs. Look at how thin she is.' Flora turned back to the bar to take another sip of her wine.

'Anyway, I'm not interested in Max Kennard,' she added belatedly, realizing that was what she should have said in the first place.

And yet there she was, glancing back at the table without meaning to, just as Max picked up his beer and glanced towards the bar, and their eyes met for a jarring second that seemed to plunge them both into a pool of stillness, cut off from the noise and laughter of the rest of the pub so effectively that Flora could only hear the buzzing in her ears and the thud of her heart. Even Ally beside her had receded behind some invisible wall.

Then someone moved and the line of sight was broken. Flora buried her nose in her glass, mortified to have been caught staring.

'What was that about?' asked Ally, who missed nothing.

'Nothing,' said Flora.

'It looked like something to me.'

'Well, it isn't. Max has got no interest in me, and he's not my type either.

What are you doing?' she added, puzzled, when Ally peered behind her.

'Just checking to see whether your pants are on fire, and let me tell you, Floradear, they are definitely smouldering.'

Flora couldn't help laughing. 'Stop it! It's true!'

'Okay, I totally believe you,' said Ally with mock earnestness. 'You've so over that crush. You've got no interest in Max Kennard at all. None. Zero. Zip. Got it.'

Flora shoved at her lightly. 'Oh, shut up. Or rather, don't. Tell me what you want to talk to Hope about instead.'

★ ★ ★

'Good morning!' Flora looked up with a smile when Max went into the kitchen on the following Monday. She was looking annoyingly bright and cheerful, the professional-looking apron wrapped neatly over a lurid orange top, and she was dicing carrots with breathtaking speed and precision.

At least, Max assumed that was what was taking his breath away. He certainly hoped it was nothing to do with the blueness of her eyes or the warm curve of her mouth.

Whatever it was only added to the scratchy, prickly, edgy feeling that had dogged him all weekend. Ever since dinner with Cressida at the Three Bells, in fact.

It hadn't been a successful evening. Max blamed Flora. When he first met Cressida, he had liked the fact that she was so tastefully dressed and restrained, but on Friday night she had seemed a little . . . *colourless*. She was pleasant, though, Max reminded himself.

Perhaps she was too impressed by the fact that he was a baronet, but at least she wasn't provocative. She didn't spend half a morning making a cup of coffee. She didn't roll her eyes at him or criticize him.

She didn't have a husky laugh that drifted through the crowds and seemed to caress the back of his neck. A laugh that whispered over his skin and uncurled in dreams that had left him stirred and unsatisfied and in a thoroughly bad mood.

All in all, dinner with Cressida would have been fine if a certain someone hadn't been perched there at the bar, Max couldn't help thinking. Somehow it had been impossible to ignore Flora. Probably because of that bright top she wore. He couldn't honestly accuse her of trying to draw attention to herself, but it was hard to concentrate on Cressida when Flora had been sitting there with Ally. They weren't shouting or screaming. They were just having a conversation and enjoying themselves. Nothing wrong with that.

They were just . . . distracting.

They had made a striking pair. Ally Parker had always been a pretty girl, and Flora was . . . vivid, Max decided, was the best way to describe her. She wasn't beautiful, she wasn't even particularly pretty, but there was a vibrancy about her, a lushness and a warmth, that made everyone around her seem just a little muted in comparison.

And clearly he hadn't been the only one to think so, Max remembered morosely. Pete Harmon, the landlord, who Max had always liked until then, had put his arms round Ally and Flora at the same time and called them his 'favourite girls' — although no prizes for guessing that his wife didn't feel the same. Both girls had hugged him back, obviously delighted to see him. Lucky Pete, Max had found himself thinking, and his hand tightened around his glass of beer while Cressida gushed about Hasebury Hall and how she had once spent a whole afternoon dreaming in the gardens. Or possibly reading in the gardens: Max had rather lost the thread of the conversation by then.

He had forced himself to concentrate on Cressida, but Flora kept tugging at the edges of his vision. She and Ally were clearly having a great time. They were greeted by almost everybody who came into the pub, and there was much hugging and kissing; and then there were the other men, lurking, jockeying for attention. Both girls were clearly lively and popular. Everything he could never be.

Or would ever want to be, Max reminded himself quickly. His parents had both been lively and popular and intensely sociable, and look where that had got them.

'Yes, I'm fine, thank you, and yes, I did have a lovely weekend, actually. Thank you so much for asking, Bella.' Belatedly, Max tuned in to the fact that Flora was talking pointedly to the dogs, who were watching her, tails wagging doubtfully, unsure what was required but willing to please. 'And how about you? Did you have some nice walks? Crunch up some bones with those big teeth of yours? You did? Excellent. And what about you, Ted? Oh, right, you don't answer either. Just like your master, in fact.'

Max's glower bounced right off her. 'Obviously you *didn't* have a nice weekend,' she said to him. 'What happened? Didn't your date work out?'

'It wasn't a *date*,' he growled. 'It was just . . . dinner.'

Flora opened her blue eyes wide. 'It looked like a date to me,' she said provocatively as she scraped the carrots into a bowl and picked up an onion, peeling and chopping it with alarming competence. No one should be able to wield a knife with that level of expertise.

'I'm surprised you noticed,' he said sourly. 'I could hardly hear what Cressida was saying over all the cackling at the bar.'

'Wow, somebody's cranky this morning!'

Max sucked in a short, irritable breath and then let it out more slowly. 'I'm sorry,' he said after a moment. 'I'm not in a good mood this morning.'

'You don't say!' She glanced at him. 'Would a coffee make it better?'

'It might.'

Flora smiled. 'Let me just put these on to sweat, then I'll make some coffee.'

5

Max watched as she added the finely diced onions to the pan and gave it a shake. 'Aren't you baking today?'

'No, I'm trying out something for the wedding — tweaking the recipe for a rosemary and redcurrant reduction that I think might go very nicely with medallions of lamb. It's just a possibility for now, of course.'

He sighed. 'Don't talk to me about that wedding!'

'Why, what's happened?'

'I've just had Hope on the phone. Apparently Jonas's sister-in-law, who's the Crown Princess and basically top dog over there, is giving her grief about seating plans.'

Flora reached into the fridge for the coffee beans and sent him a mystified look as she crossed to the coffee machine. '*Seating plans?*'

'That's what I said.' Max propped himself against the counter to watch the competent way she operated the machine. He really should learn how to do it himself, but his eyes kept drifting away from what she was doing to her profile, to the tilting corners of her mouth, along the warm line of her jaw to where it met her throat and — He looked closer. 'Please tell me those aren't bananas hanging from your ears!'

'Aren't they cute?' Flora shook her head from side to side, which set the earrings swinging. 'Ally gave them to me.'

'They look ridiculous.'

'Oh, stop with the flattery. I would have worn my diamonds, of course, but I'm having them cleaned. And anyway, a style guru like you knows that diamonds are so last season.' She clipped the puck into the machine. 'So what's the issue with the seating plans, anyway?'

'Apparently this Crown Princess Anna is very keen on protocol, and she's getting all wound up about the fact that

I'm single and that means she won't be able to arrange the tables so that they go boy-girl-boy-girl. Or something. Hope explained it to me, but to be honest I lost interest at 'seating plan'. But the upshot is that the entire principality will apparently collapse into disorder if I don't have a partner for the family meeting and announcement of the engagement in San Michele in February.'

'It sounds like this Anna or whatever her name is needs to get a life,' said Flora.

'I couldn't agree more, and so does Hope, but she's obviously been sucked into the argument and I could tell that she was upset. I think the whole royal thing is getting to her.'

'It must be tough.' Flora handed him his coffee and he thanked her as she turned back to make one for herself. 'I mean, it sounds like a fairy tale, marrying a prince and living in a palace, but how much fun can it be having to behave yourself the whole time and worry about protocol?'

'Quite. I'm worried about how Hope's going to deal with it all. She's already getting into a state about keeping the Crown Princess happy and we haven't even got to the official engagement, let alone the wedding, not to mention the reality of being married. I don't want to make things worse by refusing to take someone,' he said. 'It doesn't seem a lot for her to ask.'

Flora leant companionably against the counter beside him and sipped her own coffee, some frothy, creamy confection. 'Do you think I'm going to have find a partner too? I'm a bridesmaid so I suppose I'll be on the seating plan somewhere.' She grimaced. 'I hope not.'

Max thought of all the men clustered around her on Friday night. 'You don't have a boyfriend you can ask?'

She shook her head. 'I've sworn off men since my last boyfriend.'

There was a milky moustache on her upper lip. Max watched her run her tongue unselfconsciously over it to lick it away, and his throat dried. He coughed to clear it.

'Who was that?' he asked. Was that squeezed voice really his? 'Someone local?'

'No, I met Rich in London. I did the whole 'falling passionately in love' thing,' she said lightly, although Max guessed it was an effort. 'We moved in together and for a while it was great. Rich is a chef, and like me he was working most evenings, so we didn't have to explain to each other about the unsociable hours. He's brilliant, a bit driven and obsessive, but he can be huge fun.'

'In my experience, brilliant people are rarely fun all the time.'

'No,' she agreed. 'It was quite a lot of work to keep Rich happy, I realize now. He's hyperactive, and needs constant stimulation. If he's not cooking, he wants to be off trying other food or sourcing ingredients or talking about a possible television show . . . ' Flora sipped her coffee, remembering. 'It was exciting, but if we did sometimes have an evening off together Rich always wanted to go out and find somewhere new to eat. I love food, and I love eating out and trying new dishes too, but there were times when all I wanted was to slob on the sofa, watching telly in my pyjamas.'

Max listened in disbelief as she told him about how wonderful Rich had been. He sounded a complete tosser to Max. What kind of man chose to go out and spend a fortune on a lot of poncey rabbit food when he could be comfortable on a sofa with Flora?

And Flora in pyjamas, too. It was disturbing just how vividly he could imagine it. She would be soft and lusciously curved. Max wanted to imagine her in ivory silk, but that wouldn't be Flora. No, the pyjamas would be scarlet or hot pink, and if you put an arm around her, the slippery material would shift over her warm skin, and when you slid your hands beneath it, she would forget whatever she was watching on television and smile and wriggle round to climb on top of you and . . . and . . . dear God, where was he?

Pyjamas . . . television . . . eating out . . . With difficulty, Max dragged his attention back to the conversation, appalled at how easily his mind had veered out of control. He really must get a grip.

Flora had stopped talking. She had lost him at pyjamas . . . no, don't go there again, Max instructed himself firmly. He cleared his throat again and dredged up a memory of a previous conversation.

'This is the same boyfriend who gave you an ultimatum to choose him or your grandfather?'

'Yes,' she admitted with a sigh. She put down her cup. 'You don't need to tell me. I'm not good at picking them.'

'Well, I can't talk. I'm divorced.'

'Still, I'm sure it won't be a problem to find a partner for Hope's wedding,' said Flora. 'You can take Cressida.'

'I don't think that would be appropriate,' said Max austerely.

'Why on earth not?' Flora gave the vegetables in the pan a stir. 'She looks the part, and you said yourself that she was very nice. There'd be no risk of her eating her peas off her knife or anything, either. She looked very well-behaved.'

'It's not that.' Max hunched a shoulder. 'It's more . . . taking her as my partner to the family party might be awkward. I hardly know her, after all.'

'The party in San Michele isn't until February. There's plenty of time to get to know her.'

'That's just it. If we keep going out and getting to know each other, before we know where we are, we'll be in a relationship, and it's only a step then to expectations being raised and hints being dropped about marriage . . . It doesn't seem fair to go through all of that and then tell her I only need her with me at the wedding to keep some Crown Princess happy.'

Flora winced. 'Ouch. No, that wouldn't be good.'

'Quite. The last thing I want is for

anyone to think I'm in the market for getting married again.'

'I can't believe it would be that hard to find someone to produce as your squeeze,' she said after a moment. 'It's not as if it's a hard sell. For heaven's sake: a week in gorgeous San Michele in February, a week guzzling champagne and eating amazing meals and staying in a fairy-tale castle, a ringside seat at a royal wedding . . . What's not to like? And in return, all she'd have to do would be to sit next to you and smile for a few photos. Please! You'll be beating them off, Max. I'd do it myself if I wasn't going anyway.'

With a final stir of the pan, Flora went over to the fridge and started rummaging around for the mustard. Some Worcestershire sauce too, perhaps?

Her head in the fridge, it took her a while to realize that there was silence behind her. Straightening with the mustard in her hand, she turned to see Max watching her with a very peculiar expression.

'What?' she said.

'Why don't you?' he said slowly.

'Why don't I what?'

'Come to San Michele as my girlfriend.'

Flora laughed. 'I was joking!'

'I'm not.'

Flora looked behind her in case he was talking to some other woman secreted in the fridge.

'You want *me* to be your girlfriend?' she said carefully, still half convinced that she had misheard him.

'To *pretend* to be,' he corrected with unflattering speed. 'You said it yourself: all that's required is a show. We'd just need to turn up, look suitably affection-ate, sit through a few dinners; and then when it came to the wedding, smile for some photos. How hard could that be?'

'Yes, but . . . ' Flora stopped. 'Are you serious?'

'The more I think about it, the better an idea I think it is.' Levering himself up from the counter, Max began to pace around the kitchen. 'You're single;

I'm single. We're solving the Crown Princess's seating plan in one fell swoop. Nobody's going to be hurt if we seem to be spending time together. Plus, you're going anyway, so it's not like I need to fill you in on the situation. You know Hope. And you're not going to have any false expectations of me. You've made it clear that you don't want to stay in Combe St Philip, so I don't have any worries that you're harbouring a secret yearning to be lady of the manor.'

Belatedly realizing that the fridge door was still wide open, Flora closed it. 'Delicious as you are, my dreams lie elsewhere,' she agreed.

'Exactly! But you're committed to the wedding in any case. I think it could work, don't you?'

'Honestly, no.'

Max looked taken aback. 'Why not?'

'Well, for a start, I don't look like someone who'd be your girlfriend. Don't give me that look,' she added when he said nothing. 'You know perfectly well what I mean. You like your women beautiful and dainty and elegant, and I don't qualify on any count.'

'The Crown Princess isn't going to know that,' he pointed out.

'That's one response,' she agreed. 'Another might be: 'Oh, but you *are* beautiful and elegant, Flora, and I'm tired of having to bend down to whisper sweet nothings in fairy-like ears'.'

'I'm sorry, I might not be a style guru, but there's no way you can be described as elegant,' said Max, eyeing her top with disfavour.

'Right. You could always say that you don't care about the way I dress because I'm so incredibly sexy I don't need clothes.'

His expression didn't change, but his eyes darkened. 'I could say that, yes,' he said slowly, and something warm and dark rolled through the air, making Flora's cheeks burn.

'Or,' she hurried on, unwilling to let him see that he had flustered her, 'you could say that I've got such a sweet personality that it blinds you to my wardrobe.'

'Hmm. Not sure that 'sweet' describes you. I could say opposites attract,' Max offered, getting into the spirit of things.

'That's true.' Flora pretended to be struck by the thought. 'That's the only way anyone could possibly believe that we were compatible when I'm fun and passionate, and you're grouchy and buttoned-up.'

'I am not buttoned-up!'

'Come on, Max. When was the last time you let yourself go?'

There was a pause. 'Why don't I let myself go now?' said Max.

He came over to take the mustard from Flora's suddenly nerveless hand, put it on the worktop, and backed her gently against the fridge.

'We could practise for the Crown Princess.'

'Practise what?' Flora managed with difficulty.

She could step away easily — she

101

knew that — but her lungs seemed to have forgotten how to work, tangling up her breath. Was she supposed to be breathing in or breathing out? The lack of oxygen was doing weird things to her brain, weakening her knees and her will, making it hard to be sensible and push him away with a laugh, making her blood thud and thump with anticipation instead.

Because Max was standing very close, close enough for her to see the flecks in his green eyes, every crease fanning out at their corners, to see the faint hint of stubble along his jaw, and smell his clean, male scent.

'Looking compatible,' Max explained. 'Hmm,' he added, registering her height as if for the first time. 'I'm not used to looking a woman in the eyes at this point.'

He could only be two or three inches taller than she was, and it put their eyes almost on the same level.

Flora's heart was slamming uncomfortably against her ribs, and she moistened her lips. 'Is that a problem?'

'Far from it,' said Max. 'It's very ... convenient. And, of course, it makes it easier to see what you're thinking.'

With a heroic effort, Flora kept her eyes steady on his, but his mouth snagged tantalizingly at the edges of her vision. She would just have to lean forward an inch, maybe two, to press her lips against his and see whether they were as cool and firm as they looked. His mouth was perfectly positioned for a kiss; in fact, so close that it would be rude not to, really. She felt as if she were standing on the top of a precipitous slope, unsure whether she wanted to launch herself off for the sheer thrill of it or step back to safety, and her heart was pounding with a mixture of terror and temptation.

'And what am I thinking?' she asked bravely.

'You're thinking that I won't be able to let go. You're trying to decide whether you want me to let go or not.'

It wasn't Max's self-control she was worried about; it was her own; but he was uncannily close so, afraid he would read even more in her eyes, she let her gaze slide away from his. And the only place to look was that mouth, so cool, so inviting, so tantalizingly close.

Flora swallowed hard. 'Perhaps.'

'Well, let's try it, shall we?'

'Might as well,' she said huskily. 'Since we're here.'

His mouth curved, creasing one cheek, and heat bloomed deep inside Flora as he lifted a hand to brush his thumb along the line of her jaw. Every nerve ending in her skin seared and prickled in response. The pulse booming in her ears made it hard to think, and when he slid his hand around to the nape of her neck, she gave in and closed her eyes.

Impossible then to tell whether he tugged her towards him or she leant in to him, but their lips touched with a bright shock of recognition that pushed Flora over the edge into a dark, delicious slide of sheer sensation: the warmth of his fingers, the solid strength of his body, the faint lingering taste of coffee. The kiss was gently explorative at first, but their lips fitted together so well that the pleasure bloomed into heat, and that in turn spiralled insistently into a fiercer need to discover more, to press closer, to taste deeper.

Flora's hair tickled the back of Max's hand as it curved at the nape of her neck. The clean, summery scent that was particularly hers filled his head. Her skin was as warm as he had imagined it, and she was soft and pliant, melting into him so that they seemed to fit each other perfectly, like two pieces of a jigsaw you hadn't considered together suddenly clicking into place.

He had intended a light-hearted kiss, just to show Flora that he wasn't as buttoned-up as she thought; but no sooner did her lips open under his than the slow simmer between them rose to the boil and surged between them, and he was lost. There was nothing but her warm, responsive body, the softness of her skin, the sweetness of her mouth, the low purr of pleasure in her throat. Light-headed, Max pressed closer, one hand still cupping her head, the other skimming her curves, frantically searching for a way under the garish top so that he could explore the lush warmth beneath.

Bella chose that moment to utter a sharp, disapproving bark and shove her head between them. Max so nearly pushed her firmly away with his leg, but she had reminded him where he was, curse her, and though his heart thundered still, his mind cleared enough for him to realize just where this was going unless one of them was sensible. And, as always, it looked as if it was going to have to be him.

Reluctantly, he withdrew his hand, and let his mouth trail apologetically along Flora's jaw to kiss the frantically beating pulse below her ear, nearly losing his resolve when she tipped her head back with a shudder of desire.

'We're embarrassing Bella,' he murmured against her neck, his voice tattered with frustration, and felt Flora remember where she was too. She stiffened as he levered himself away from her with an effort, and her eyes when she opened them were a dark, dazed blue.

Her hand went to her throat. 'Good timing, Bella,' she said, and Max was ridiculously glad that her voice was no steadier than his had been.

'I think we should be able to convince the Crown Princess, don't you?' he said.

6

Flora's knees were so weak that she was glad of the fridge at her back as Max stepped away, looking infuriatingly cool. How could he kiss her like that and then look so calm? She'd had to practically unpeel herself from him, to stop the hands that were busily dragging his shirt from his trousers in a frantic search to reach his skin, to feel the sleek strength of his back beneath her palms, while *Max* . . . Max was sounding a little ragged, perhaps, but seemed amused, while she was still reeling with stunned disbelief at how utterly she had lost control.

If it had been simple pleasure in touch and feel, that would have been one thing, but it had felt more complicated than that: the pleasure, yes, but a sense of coming home, too, the thrill of the unknown, the throb of hunger for more and more. Flora wanted to stamp her feet at the unfairness of it.

Take it lightly, she told herself fiercely, as she struggled to compose her expression. Pleading for him to kiss her again would be so uncool. 'I suppose we could carry it off,' she conceded.

'So you'll do it?'

With a huge effort, Flora levered herself upright and retrieved the mustard. 'Only if you'll pretend to be absolutely besotted with me,' she said.

Max's eyes dropped to her mouth. Flora didn't know what it looked like, but it certainly felt as if it were swollen and throbbing. 'I think I can manage that,' he said.

There was a sizzling pause. Flora stiffened her knees and turned back to open the fridge once more, which at least gave her the chance to cool her hot face.

'I think it's time we were serious,' she said when she had found the Worcester-shire sauce and judged that the treacherous tide of colour had ebbed from her face. 'Are we really going to do this? To pretend to be a couple just for the sake of a seating plan?'

'Not for a seating plan,' said Max. 'For Hope.'

'We'd have to tell her the truth,' Flora said. 'I don't want to lie to my friends. Hope needs to know that we're just pretending.'

'That's fair enough. I don't want to lie to her either, or to Holly and Ben, come to that. And if they know the truth, then Stella will have to know too. They shouldn't have secrets from their own mother.'

'Okay. So we tell Hope, Holly, Ben and Stella — and Ally,' Flora remembered. 'If Hope knows, then Ally has to know too.'

'Why don't we tell Jennifer Harmon too and make sure the whole of the Three Bells knows? It's not going to be much of a pretence.'

'There's no need to be sarcastic,' Flora said with dignity. 'Ally is a good friend. And anyway, I might as well tell her, because she'd see through any pretence in a second.'

'Very well.' Max was suddenly all business. 'So, we're agreed. We'll go to San Michele and the wedding as a couple to save Hope from any more grief from the Crown Princess?'

Flora took a deep breath and told herself not to think about how it had felt to kiss him. 'All right,' she said. 'We'll do it for Hope.'

★   ★   ★

After the long plod through November and the first week of December, suddenly Christmas was looming. Lights were strung across the high street in Ayesborough and the shops played a relentless soundtrack of Christmas music. Flora's whimsical Yule logs and beautifully decorated Christmas cakes were in high demand from local cafés, and her days passed in a frenzy of pastry-making for the mince pies that were flying off the shelves as fast as she could bake them.

She was glad to be busy. It meant there was no time to think about that kiss, and she fell into bed every night too tired to dream.

Which was just as well.

To Flora's annoyance, Max treated her exactly as he had done before. In other words, he was grouchy, sardonic or austerely aloof. It should have been easy to forget how warm his mouth had felt against hers, how hungrily those capable hands had explored her. It should have been easy to wipe out the memory of that spiralling pleasure, to dismiss the kiss as a joke or a test or completely meaningless, the way Max had so obviously done.

But it wasn't.

Every time Max walked into the kitchen, Flora's pulse spiked, and her stomach tipped and her heart did that silly somersault. It was ridiculous.

Max had rung Hope that night to tell her what they had agreed, and Hope called Flora the moment he had put the phone down.

'Flora, I'm so grateful to you,' she had said, 'but are you sure about it? Max *says* it's just a pretence.'

The question hung in the air. Outside, the wind was blowing around the cottage chimney. The fire was lit, the curtains drawn, and Sweetie was installed on her lap. Having made himself comfortable, he was refusing to move, and if Flora shifted at all, he would dig his claws into her thighs in punishment.

'Of course it is,' said Flora firmly. She had almost been able to convince herself that the kiss was already halfway to being forgotten. 'Honestly, Hope, it's no big deal. We're both going to be in San Michele anyway, so we thought we'd save you some hassle, that's all.'

'Well, I can't tell you what a relief it is to be able to tell Anna that it's all sorted. I know how silly it all sounds, but it was turning into a nightmare.' Hope paused. 'So, you and Max . . . ? I never thought of you together before, but as soon as Max said it, it made perfect sense.'

'Hope, it's just *pretend*,' Flora reminded her.

'Oh, yes, sure,' said Hope airily. Too airily. It was almost as if she hadn't believed Flora. 'I'm really excited about February now that I know you're coming with Max and the kids.'

'I can't wait,' she told Hope, as she scratched Sweetie warily under his chin — he could lash out at any moment, as she knew to her cost — and listened to the wind buffeting the windows. 'I've forgotten what blue skies and sunshine look like.'

Hope laughed. 'You'll get plenty of that when you get to San Michele,' she promised.

She had sounded so happy that Flora was reassured. It might be a mad plan, but she and Max were doing the right thing.

She had forgotten, though, how many other people were involved once you started to lie. Max had certainly been quick to tell Stella about the plan. Much to Flora's surprise, Stella had been all for it.

'It's good for Max to get the idea of having someone else in his life,' she confided to Flora when she dropped Holly and Ben off one Thursday. 'I do worry about him rattling around in this old house on his own.'

You should have stayed married to him, in that case, Flora wanted to say, but she wisely kept her mouth shut and determinedly rolled out pastry instead. Looking at Stella's perfect features, at the pansy eyes and glossy hair and delicate figure, it was depressing to realize just how easy it must have been for Max to wipe Flora's kiss out of his mind. How could kissing *her* have meant anything to him when he must remember kissing Stella every time he saw his beautiful ex-wife? Flora had provoked him, he had risen to the challenge, and that was all there was to it.

She was pretty sure that Stella was

only being so positive about the whole business because she knew that Flora was absolutely no threat.

Stella had accepted a cup of tea ('no milk for me, thanks') while Holly and Ben devoured a lemon drizzle cake Flora had made especially for them.

'You make brilliant cakes,' said Ben loyally, chasing the last crumb around his plate. 'We're having a cake stall at school to raise money for charity. Can you make some for me to take?'

'Ben! Darling! I've already said I'll buy you some cakes for the stall.'

'But Flora's cakes are better,' Ben protested.

'I don't mind,' Flora put in quickly when Stella's delicate brows drew together in displeasure. 'I'd be happy to make you some cakes, Ben.'

'Cool.' Ben went back to his computer game, evidently considering that no more needed to be said.

'Just like his father!' Stella managed a silvery laugh. 'Thank you so much, Flora. You must let me know how much the ingredients cost.'

'It's not a problem, really,' said Flora uncomfortably. She liked Ben, who was indeed shaping up to be as taciturn as Max, but who ate everything she made with frank appreciation. He looked straight at you and said what he thought if you asked him, but otherwise took little part in a conversation.

'It's a good idea, Mummy.' Unusually, Holly spoke up in support of her brother. 'Everyone will want to buy a cake if they know Flora made it, because she's a proper cook, so the stall will make more money. And if they know she's made it for Ben, they won't be surprised when they hear that Flora's going out with Daddy.'

'*Pretending* to go out with him,' Flora said quickly.

'Will you come to my dance event, Flora?' Holly went on without bothering to acknowledge fine distinctions. 'I'm going to be doing a solo,' she added proudly. 'I'm a dragonfly.'

'Wow, I can't miss that,' said Flora,

although she sensed that Stella wasn't entirely pleased.

It was strange being involved in village activities again. Flora had spent the previous two Christmases with her grandfather, but he hadn't been well enough to go out. They had even missed the midnight service on Christmas Eve that had always been such a big part of Christmas when she was growing up. Before that, she had been in London most Christmases, caught up in the frantic rush of a restaurant kitchen and the buzz of the city in festive mood, but always managing a quick dash down to Combe St Philip to see her grandparents when she could.

Now London seemed a long way away. It belonged to a different world to the village pantomime in the parish hall, to the carollers on the doorstep, and the primary school's nativity play. Holly and Ben went to a private school on the other side of Ayesborough. Ben announced proudly that Flora's cakes had made a record amount of money for their charity, and when Flora turned up at Holly's dance event, she found herself besieged by requests for cakes for special occasions. One woman was desperate for Flora to make a golden wedding cake for her parents the following September.

'I'm not sure . . . ' It was a shock to Flora to realize that she might not be in the village then. She might be back in London, running her own restaurant. Her dream might have come true at last. Why was it so hard to imagine?

'Oh, please do say you will! Your cakes are so exquisite. They're like works of art. It would mean the world to my parents.'

Over the woman's shoulder, she could see Max talking to Stella and an urbane-looking man who was presumably Stella's husband, Marcus. Max had a hand on Ben's shoulder and Holly was jumping up and down with excitement, still dressed in her gauzy green dragonfly costume. Flora's chest tightened. The five of them made a family. A modern family, perhaps, but a family nonetheless.

A family she would never be part of, no matter how many cakes she made for Ben.

She turned back to the woman who was pleading with her to reconsider, and telling her all about the big family party they had planned for her parents. 'We'll all be there, including the great-grandchildren.'

What would it be like to be part of such a big family? Flora wondered. She might not belong to one, but she could at least contribute. She dug in her bag for a business card and handed it over. 'Call me in the new year,' she said, relenting. 'I'll make something special for your parents.'

At least she had made someone happy, she thought as she let herself into the cottage later that evening. Sweetie was stalking behind the door, meowing imperiously as he made his displeasure at her late arrival known. Flora fed him with abject apologies and he allowed himself to be placated, jumping onto her lap afterwards and kneading her thighs with sharp claws before turning in circles several times and curling up at last.

Flora stroked his soft fur, glad of his warmth and the sense of another beating heart in the empty cottage. Looking across at her grandfather's chair, she remembered him sitting there, remembered the twinkle in his eyes, the way his moustache had tickled her when he kissed her goodnight. The band around her chest tightened unbearably as she thought about Max and his children, all the other families gathering together at Christmas.

'Hey, I've got you,' she said to Sweetie, smiling wryly to herself as the cat ignored her completely. 'You're my family now.'

★ ★ ★

Max paused at the manor gates and whistled for the dogs. They were ecstatic at getting another walk after being shut in all day while he'd been at Stella's, and were snuffling happily in the undergrowth. As always, Christmas lunch had stretched long into the afternoon, and it had been nearly seven before he'd been able to get away. He'd walked Bella and Ted as soon as he got in, but he couldn't settle.

The truth was that he'd been restless ever since kissing Flora that day. Now he couldn't open the damned fridge for the butter without thinking about how warm she had been, how sweet she had tasted. It had been a stupid thing to do.

The cold made his teeth ache and his breath hung in frozen clouds in the air. Holly and Ben had been disappointed that once again it hadn't been a white Christmas, but Max preferred it like this. A hard frost had lent a sheen to the road, and the countryside was rigid in a starlight so bright he had no need of a torch. It was very quiet as he crossed the green, Bella and Ted quartering the grass, noses to the ground. Everyone was at home, tucked up in the warm behind closed curtains. Even the Three Bells was locked and dark. He wondered how Flora had got on.

When he had asked what she was doing for Christmas, she'd told him that she would be helping out at the pub.

'Bit of a busman's holiday, isn't it?'

'It'll be fun,' she'd said. 'The atmosphere's always great when you're cooking Christmas lunch. Even Jennifer Harmon cracks a smile.'

But now it was half past nine and everyone had gone home — even Flora, who had only a sneaky cat to go home to.

Without meaning to, his feet had taken him past the church, past the old market cross, past what had once been the village shop run by Norman and Margaret Deare, and up the street that curved round towards the lane where they had lived. It was a pretty stone cottage with steps up to the front door. In the summer, Margaret Deare had decorated the steps with a colourful display of geraniums and busy lizzies, but the pots were empty now.

The curtains were drawn but a sliver of welcoming yellow light showed through a crack. Flora was still up.

Bella and Ted waited, puzzled, by his side. Max hesitated, then knocked at the door.

There was a pause, long enough for Max to wonder what the hell he was doing. He was on the verge of turning to go, unsure whether he was relieved or disappointed, when Flora opened the door. She was wearing faded pyjama bottoms covered in pale blue bunnies and a baggy jumper that Max strongly suspected might have belonged to her grandfather. Her hair was tousled and her face a bit puffy and creased, as if she had fallen asleep on the sofa.

She looked wonderful.

Max felt his heart swell even as his tongue tangled over an explanation for what he was doing on her doorstep. 'I, er, I was passing and thought I'd wish you a happy Christmas.'

Flora looked at him for a long moment, and then she stood back to hold open the door. 'Come in.' She looked down at Bella and Ted who were pushing forward. 'I suppose you'd better come in too, but I don't know what Sweetie is going to say.'

Sweetie had plenty to say. He made it clear that he wasn't having any dogs in his house. He puffed up in a ferocious ball of black fluff and hissed so terrifyingly from the back of a chair that Bella and Ted whimpered and ran behind Max.

'Do you think they'd mind going in the kitchen?'

Max thought they'd be only too glad to get away from the cat. But by the time they'd separated the animals, and Flora had poured a glass of wine, and the cat had returned to his normal size to stalk menacingly back and forwards in front of the kitchen door, they were left with an awkward silence.

'I'm sorry, did I wake you up?'

'I think I did drop off.' She rubbed her hair. 'That's why I look such a mess. I wasn't expecting any visitors.'

'Sorry,' he said again. 'Perhaps I shouldn't have come. It was an impulse.'

And how long was it since he had given in to one of those?

'I'm glad you did,' said Flora, settling herself cross-legged on the end of the little sofa. 'It's nice to have some company. Sweetie is even less chatty than you are.'

'How was lunch in the Three Bells?' he asked stiffly.

'Great. Hectic, but worth it. We had a laugh. I love Tom,' she added with a reminiscent smile.

Max hated the way he prickled instantly at the idea. 'Tom?'

'You must know Tom!' Flora looked at Max in surprise. 'The chef at the Three Bells? He's the one who really turned it into a gastropub.'

She forgot that he didn't know Combe St Philip the way she did, Max thought. Hasebury Hall was on the outskirts of the village, set at the end of its long avenue, its boundary marked by the great stone gates his great-great-grandfather had erected. Flora might not have been born in the village, or come from a family that had dominated it for some five hundred years, but she was part of Combe St Philip in a way that he could never be, especially since his father's greed and stupidity had irretrievably ruined the reputation of the Kennards.

Flora was telling him how Pete Harmon had given her her first job at sixteen, helping in the kitchen. 'I loved it so much, I became assistant chef as soon as I left school. Tom was the one who said I should go to London a couple of years later. He said he'd taught me all he could and I needed to move on. I owe him everything. Even if I hadn't enjoyed it, I would have helped Tom out so the other staff could have a break over Christmas.'

She swirled her glass and bent her

head over it to sniff the wine appreciatively. 'So, how was your Christmas?'

'Oh, fine . . . the usual: overexcited children, too much to eat, polite conversation with Marcus.'

'Is it hard, seeing Stella with Marcus?'

'No.' Max was definite about that. 'I'm just glad she's happy now. I feel guilty about the divorce.'

Flora paused with the glass halfway to her lips. 'But I thought Stella left you?'

'She did, but I didn't make things easy for her.' Max stared down into his own glass as if he could see the past shimmering there. 'We'd only been married a year when she found herself in the middle of a national scandal when my father was arrested. It was a humiliating time, to say the least of it, and Stella was dragged down with the rest of us.'

Shame still burned in the pit of Max's stomach whenever he thought about how greedy and stupid and dishonourable his father had been. Gerald Kennard's family had had no idea of what he'd been doing, but they were tainted by association.

'Stella thought she was marrying a landscape designer in line to inherit a prosperous estate and a historic manor house. She ended up embroiled in scandal and shame and with a husband presiding over the sell-off of the family inheritance. To be honest, I'm surprised she stuck with me as long as she did.'

7

Flora didn't look convinced. 'Whatever happened to 'for better or worse'?'

'These things are never one-sided,' said Max. 'There was so much going on then. I had to cope with my mother, who shrugged off my father's betrayal, but refused to accept that she couldn't afford to live in the same way they had done. I was worried about Hope. She adored our father, and was only fifteen when her whole world turned upside down.

'In the middle of it all, Stella was pregnant,' he remembered. 'I didn't give her enough attention, and by the time Holly was born, I was in the middle of trying to rescue something from the whole mess. I was determined to save Hasebury Hall, if nothing else, but that meant I had to sell all the farms and all the land except for the gardens. The paintings and antique furniture and silver had to go, too. Cars, horses, jewellery, the lot.'

The corners of Flora's mouth pulled down. 'It must have been tough.'

'People deal with worse things. We still had a roof over our heads — just.'

Max shrugged; but it *had* been tough, disposing of everything his ancestors had worked so hard to acquire. He'd imagined them spinning furiously in their tombs in St Philip and All Angels. He'd had no choice, Max knew, but still the guilt weighed heavily on him.

'With brilliant timing, I'd set up as a freelance landscape designer two months before my father was arrested,' he told Flora. 'That was a struggle too. I realized that if I was to pay off the mountain of debts, I had to find a new source of income.'

'Is that why you set up your pot plant business?'

He nodded. 'It's not something that makes my gardener's soul thrill, I have to admit, but it's turned into a much more profitable sideline than I could have imagined, and it meant that I could hold on to Hasebury Hall and feed my family.

'But that was another thing occupying my attention, and Stella resented it. She hadn't signed up for a frugal existence, for constantly being told to save money, to put on a jumper instead of the heating. She was used to skiing holidays and summers in Tuscany and, I don't know, new clothes and whatever women spend their money on. I was preoccupied and short-tempered, which didn't help. We argued constantly about money, how she couldn't spend a hundred quid on having her hair done or to invite friends round to dinner.'

'You don't have to spend a fortune on dinner with friends,' Flora pointed out.

'You do when you insist on having it catered because you can't cook.'

'Stella can't cook?' Flora looked astounded.

'Not everyone loves food the way you do,' said Max. 'Stella would happily get by on a lettuce leaf or two, and I'm in no position to criticize her on the cooking front, I know. I can put together a spaghetti bolognaise from a jar, but that's about it.'

'What about Holly and Ben?'

'Stella's got an au pair who cooks pretty well — she did a good job of Christmas lunch, anyway. And there are always prepared meals from the super-market.' He almost smiled at Flora's expression.

'Ending a marriage is never good, but by the end, I was just glad to stop the fighting. Marcus had been waiting in the wings a long time, I think, and Stella married him very quickly after we were divorced. He gives her all the financial security she craves, and he's good with the kids, too. Holly and Ben love him. It's much better for them than growing up with Stella and me rowing the whole time.'

'Hmm,' said Flora doubtfully. 'So

Stella leaves you and ends up with the kids, an adoring husband and lots of money, while you get the debts and a house that's falling down around your ears?'

'It's not that bad,' Max couldn't help protesting. 'It just needs a little paint.'

'It doesn't seem fair.'

'It is fair,' he insisted. 'The truth is, I put saving Hasebury Hall above my marriage. That's on me. There have been Kennards at the manor for hundreds of years. I just couldn't stand the thought of being the one who let it go.'

'That would have been your father's responsibility, not yours,' Flora pointed out.

'Yes, but he didn't care about Hasebury Hall the way I did. The way I *do*. For my father, the estate was just there to fund his lifestyle, while for me, it's part of who I am.'

Max sipped reflectively at his wine. 'I learnt that from my grandfather. He was the opposite of my father: very upright, very stern and a bit forbidding to a lot of people, but he had complete integrity and he loved Hasebury Hall with a passion. Even when I was very small, he would take me round the house and we'd stop at every portrait so that he could tell me about each ancestor and what they had done for the estate.'

'I think I remember my grandparents talking about him,' said Flora. 'I've got a feeling my grandfather fought alongside him in the Second World War — though Pops was just a soldier and your grandfather an officer, of course, so he didn't really know him. But Pops admired him, I know that.'

'He wasn't an easy man to get to know. He preferred dogs to people. When they died, he buried them in a corner of the orchard and gave them a proper headstone. I knew as much about the dogs as I did about the portraits of my ancestors.'

Max half-smiled at the memory. 'He died when I was seven, but I've never forgotten him telling me that Hasebury

Hall would be mine one day and that I would have to look after it. That's what kept me going when I was sent away to school later that year.

'I hated it,' he remembered bleakly. 'I used to lie in my dorm with my head under my pillow so no one would hear me crying. All I wanted to do was to come home. I wasn't homesick for my parents, but I missed the house and the dogs. My father had a golden retriever called Bess — a love of dogs was the only thing we ever had in common — and she was a great dog. I missed her more than my parents.'

Poor little boy, thought Flora. Her throat ached for the seven-year-old Max, sent away from all that was familiar. No wonder he had seemed aloof in the village. No wonder he had fallen so heavily for Stella and the idea of someone to love him.

'Seven's very young to go away to boarding school,' she said.

'It was supposed to toughen me up,' Max said flatly. 'Besides, what else were my parents supposed to do with their child while they were off having a good time?' She could hear his struggle to erase the underlying bitterness in his voice, but his mouth twisted. 'So I'd long to come home, but when I did, I didn't really feel I belonged here either any more. My parents usually had friends staying, and I was a nuisance. I thought it would be better when Hope was born, but she was so much our father's favourite . . . ' He shrugged. 'Well, there wasn't a place for me.'

The thought of the careless cruelty to the little boy he had been made Flora tighten her fingers around the stem of her glass. 'What about your mother? Didn't she love you?'

'Oh, my mother . . . ' Max lifted his shoulders and then dropped them as if defeated by the idea of explaining his mother to anyone. 'I don't think, really, that my mother loved anyone but herself. She was beautiful and spoiled, and she could be great fun. I remember how she used to laugh, and how she'd light up a room when she walked into it, but she had the attention span of a gnat. She was made to flit around parties, not deal with messy stuff like children or money.

'She wasn't horrified by what my father had done, but she couldn't forgive him for ruining her comfortable lifestyle. She divorced him straight away and remarried a wealthy banker who could keep her in the manner to which she felt entitled.'

'She died not long after your father, didn't she?'

'Yes, swimming off some billionaire's yacht after too much champagne for lunch.' Max's smile was more painful than he realized. 'Typical of her. I can just hear her saying, 'Oh, but darling, *what* a way to go!''

Flora uncrossed her legs to lean over and refill his glass. 'It's not much fun having a mother who doesn't love you, is it?'

'No.' He looked at her. 'Do you still see yours?'

'Occasionally. She drifts in and out of my life.' Having refilled her own glass, Flora wriggled around to find a more comfortable position against the cushions and crossed her legs once more. 'Sky isn't a bad person. She can be quite charming, in fact, but I've never been enough for her. She's always searching for something *more*, something spiritual.

'A lot of what I've done is in reaction to Sky. She eats lentils and mung beans; I cook incredibly elaborate and expensive dishes. She lives in ashrams or communes; I had a loft in east London. She's slight and ethereal; I'm . . . not. I blame my grandmother for that,' Flora added with a smile. 'She was so appalled at my diet when I first came to live here that she cooked me treats the whole time. Steamed puddings were my favourite, so I had lots of those. I was skinny then, if you can believe it, but by the time I'd been here three months I was a little pudding myself!'

'Did you ever know your father?'

Max asked curiously.

'I've no idea who he was,' said Flora. 'I tried asking Sky, but she just says I was born in a 'place of great love', so I suspect she doesn't know either.' She sighed a little. 'I used to long for a father. Before I got to know Hope, I envied her so much having a father who adored her. But I was lucky,' she added quickly. 'Pops was the perfect father figure for me.'

It was almost as if she wouldn't let herself acknowledge the sadness in her story. Max thought about his own father, who had humiliated and betrayed them. At least he had known who his father was and where he came from. Flora didn't even have that.

Flora ran a finger around the rim of her glass, thinking about her mother. 'For a long time, I resented her. It wasn't so much the way she ignored me, as the way she never thought about my grandparents. It used to make me furious, but I realized when Pops was ill that actually, it was my mother's loss. I got to spend time with him, and she didn't. So I managed to let all that go in the end — although I still can't forgive her for my name,' she added, thinking that it was time to lighten the atmosphere.

'What's wrong with Flora?' Max asked, surprised.

'It's not the name on my birth certificate.'

He sat up. 'What is?'

Flora pressed her lips together and shook her head. 'I could tell you, but then I'd have to kill you.'

'Tell me.'

'You'll laugh.'

Max pointed at his face. 'Does this look like the face of a man who would laugh at you?'

She let her eyes rest on the austere angles of his cheek and jaw, the heart-shakingly cool line of his mouth, and the memory of the kiss they had shared flared bright inside her. She looked away.

'Do you promise you won't tell

anyone? Even Hope doesn't know.'

'Cross my heart and hope to die. What should I be calling you?'

'Moonflower Dreaming.'

There was a silence. Looking up from her glass, Flora saw the edges of his mouth twitch very slightly. 'I knew you'd laugh!'

With a heroic effort, Max kept his face straight. I'm not laughing. It's . . . unusual.'

'I can't tell you how many times I wished I was called Mary or Michelle or something normal.'

'How did you get to be Flora?'

'Sky brought me to visit my grandparents here when I was eight. We'd been living in various communes up to then. They were always cold, always faintly grubby.' Flora gestured around the cosy room. 'It's not very big, but coming here was like stumbling into paradise. Sky was talking about following some guru to India, and Granny and Pops persuaded her to leave me with them so that I could go to school.

'I suspect Sky was already finding that I was cramping her style,' she said. 'My grandparents thought I'd be upset that she would go away and leave me, but I couldn't believe how lucky I was. They said I could have my very own room, all to myself, and I got to choose the wallpaper and they bought me a Cinderella nightlight.'

Her face was soft with memory. 'Then they sat me down and suggested that they call me Flora instead of Moonflower Dreaming and I was so grateful that I'd have agreed to anything they said. I was glad, anyway, when I got to school. It was bad enough having a 'weird' mother without having a weird name as well. I've been Flora ever since.'

'Am I really the only one who knows you're actually called Moonflower Dreaming?' asked Max, and Flora nodded.

'I didn't even tell Rich,' she said, and when she glanced at him almost shyly, their gazes snared and tangled, and something more complicated shimmered into life in the air between them.

Something that thickened Max's blood and set his heart thudding painfully. Flora was sitting on the sofa in those ratty old clothes, looking lush and warm and impossibly inviting. He wanted to peel off that awful jumper and slide her beneath him onto the cushions, wanted to explore the shadowy hollow between her breasts, to skim his lips over every dip and curve of her, to taste her and feel her and hear her sigh with pleasure.

He drained his wine and stood up before he had a chance to change his mind. 'I'd better go,' he said.

'Oh. Right.' Flora blinked a little at the abrupt change of mood, but she uncurled herself from the sofa.

Max rescued Bella and Ted from the kitchen. They scuttled out of the front door rather than face the cat who hissed contemptuously after them.

Flora hugged her arms together in the open doorway as Max turned on the doorstep.

'Thanks for the wine.'

'Thanks for coming.'

He should say goodbye. He should step back and go. He should absolutely not touch her. But something about Flora's smile made his breath snag in his throat, and Max did what he had been wanting to do all evening, all day, ever since he had kissed her in the kitchen in fact. Instead of stepping back, he stepped forward and cupped his hands around her face so that he could kiss her.

It was like diving into warmth, into a rush and a swirl of pleasure. He felt her hands uncross to clutch at his waist as her mouth opened beneath his, and he pulled her closer, lost in the pounding surge of his blood until from somewhere he found the willpower to ease away and drop a last kiss on her parted lips.

'Happy Christmas, Moonflower Dreaming,' he said.

8

It was the beginning of January, and the Christmas decorations around the village were looking tired and tatty. Outside Max's study window, the sky was a bleak grey. Almost as bleak as the way he felt.

He hadn't seen Flora since Christmas night. He'd tried to call round at the cottage a few times, because it wasn't the kind of thing you could discuss on the phone, but either she'd been out or he'd had the children, and somehow here they were in January and they still hadn't talked about that kiss.

About either kiss.

But Flora was back in the kitchen today. He was squinting at bank statements in the hope of making the figures at the end somehow different, when he heard her let herself in at the back door, and in spite of himself, his heart lifted, just knowing that she was near.

Which was completely ridiculous, and he needed to deal with it as soon as possible. Max took off his glasses, pushed back his chair, and strode through the great hall and down the passage to the kitchen.

Flora was tying her apron round her waist, but she looked up with a bright smile when he came in. 'Happy New Year!' she said.

'Where have you been?' he barked at her, and she lifted her brows in faint surprise.

'I went to stay with friends in London for New Year. I just got back last night.'

'Oh.' Max was unreasonably deflated. Had he really thought she would sit around moping and waiting for him to call? 'Good time?' he asked.

'Fabulous. Although I wish I hadn't remembered what a hangover feels like. We went to a fantastic party on New Year's Eve — I'd forgotten how much I like dancing.'

'I thought you couldn't leave that cat of yours?' said Max grumpily.

'I can leave him for a few days. I just can't up sticks and sell the cottage. Ally's mother fed him, in case you were worried about him.' She clicked on the coffee machine. 'How about you? What did you do for New Year?'

'I had the kids here. We took a picnic and walked over the downs to Avebury on New Year's Day.'

Which sounded a bit sad compared to a London party with dancing. Not that Max wouldn't rather stick needles in his eyes than go to a party with dancing, but it just underscored the differences between them. Obviously Flora wouldn't want to tramp over the downs with two children, even if Holly and Ben had enjoyed themselves after the initial obligatory moaning.

'What did you have in your picnic?'

Max stared at her in disbelief. Only Flora would be interested. 'Cheese and pickle sandwiches,' he said and she shook her head.

'That's not a picnic. That's a sandwich.'

'I suppose you were eating caviar and filet mignon, whatever that is,' he said morosely.

'Not exactly. But it was a chance to try some new restaurants and pick up new ideas.' She handed him the coffee she had made without asking. 'I think I may have changed my mind about the wedding starter.'

'Thanks.' Max took the cup and waited until she had her own. 'I missed coffee like this when you were away,' he confessed.

I missed you. That's what he should have said. That was what he meant.

Flora leant easily back against the counter. 'You know, you could learn how to use the machine. It's really not complicated.'

He knew she was right. He could have used the machine instead of reverting to instant coffee, but the kitchen hadn't felt comfortable without her, and he'd avoided it as much as possible. The manor that had once been his haven had been empty and cold, just an old stone building without any warmth at its heart. Holly and Ben had grumbled that it wasn't the same without Flora, and even the dogs had been moping.

'So.' Max cleared his throat. 'I really came down to apologize.'

'Apologize?' Flora echoed in surprise. 'What on earth for?'

He put down his cup on the counter and set his jaw. 'For kissing you on Christmas night.'

'Oh, *that*.'

All this time he had been fretting about the kiss, either wondering whether to apologize for it or pretend it had never happened, while simultaneously doing his level best to put it out of his mind completely, and all it had meant to Flora was 'that'.

'Honestly, Max, don't give it another thought,' Flora said. 'It was just one of those things. Both of us alone on Christmas night, a glass of wine . . . it's easy to get carried away. But I know it didn't mean anything, so you really don't need to explain, and certainly not to apologize.'

It might not have meant anything to her, but he had spent the whole week obsessing about it, thought Max, aggrieved. He knew he ought to be grateful she wasn't making a big deal out of it, but he wasn't feeling grateful. He was feeling a fool.

'I wouldn't want it to cause any awkwardness,' he said stiffly.

'It isn't awkward. At least not for me.'

'Right. Good.'

'The thing is, I think we both know it's not a good idea to get involved in any way,' Flora went on. 'Especially as we're having to spend so much time together between now and the wedding. I can't afford to give up using this lovely kitchen, for a start, and if we got together and then it didn't work out — well, then it *would* be awkward. And it's not as if we'd ever have a serious relationship.'

'No,' said Max.

'Going back to London for New Year

was good for me. It reminded me of where I really want to be.'

Great. He was so pleased for her. Max scowled down into his coffee.

'Which isn't to say it wasn't a nice kiss,' Flora added kindly.

Nice. Was that all it had been for her?

'But we both know that we could never have a future together. We've got nothing in common. I'll be going back to London as soon as I can, and you're committed to Combe St Philip. Even if it wasn't for how you feel about the manor, your children are here.'

All of which was exactly what Max had said to himself countless times since Christmas night. He had been going to make all those arguments himself to make her see that it wouldn't be a good idea to take things any further. So he should have been delighted that Flora had saved him the trouble.

Funny, he didn't *feel* delighted.

'You're right,' he said. 'It would be a very bad idea.'

'Exactly.'

'I'm just glad you're not upset. I didn't want you to feel that I'd . . . taken advantage of you.'

'I'm a big girl, Kennard. If I hadn't wanted you to kiss me, I could have said no. But it was just a kiss. We don't need to make a big deal out of it.'

'Good,' said Max. 'Well, I'd be glad to forget it if you will.'

'Already forgotten,' she assured him with a brilliant smile.

The moment Max had left, the smile dropped from Flora's face and she slumped against the counter, exhausted by the effort of pretending to be upbeat and unaffected.

Lust and confusion had kept her awake all of Christmas night after that devastating kiss. It had been so . . . so *perfect*. Like two interlocking pieces of a puzzle fitting together, clicking into place with an 'aha!' of realization about how things were supposed to go.

It would be so easy to fall in love with Max. Flora felt as if she were teetering on the brim of a dizzyingly deep chasm. Because it might be easy to fall in love, but she could already see how hard it would be to get herself out. And nothing had really changed. He was still bound up with Stella, bound up with his children and his dogs and the manor and everything that was nothing to do with her, while she had her own plans. They might be on hold while Sweetie was still alive, but the day would come when she would be free to pursue her dream of having a restaurant. There would be no point in tangling that up with a man who was always going to be emotionally unavailable.

However warm his hands. However good it felt to lean in to him. However heart-shaking his kiss.

It had been a good idea to go to London, and she *had* had a good time. She had hardly thought about Max at all. No more than two or three (okay, twenty or thirty) times a day.

She had danced all night long on New Year's Eve, and when midnight struck she wouldn't let herself imagine being alone with him at the manor, curled up on a sofa in front of the fire, crawling over him to kiss her way along his jaw and down his throat, letting his hands roam over her, feeling him smiling that rare and heart-stopping smile against her skin.

Or not much.

She had kissed friends and hugged random strangers instead, and drunk too much cheap wine, and the next morning she had felt vile.

She could have been walking along the ancient trackways with Max and his children. The sky was always bigger up there. When the wind was blowing on the ridgeway it was like flying above the lovely sweeps of the open downland, looking down over the immaculately tilled fields and copses, and the villages tucked into the valley. They could have sat on the old, old stones and had a proper picnic, not just a measly cheese and pickle sandwich. It would have been fun.

Flora sighed.

It would be a very bad idea: wasn't that what Max had said? He had been grim-faced and obviously terrified that she would get all emotional and make too much out of that kiss. At least she'd been able to keep smiling and act as if she didn't care, when every cell in her body had been screaming at her to throw herself into his arms and beg him to kiss her again. Thank God she had been able to hold on to some shreds of pride.

The next six months would be about Hope and giving her the wedding of her dreams. Pretending to be Max's girl-friend was part of that, but it would be a big mistake to muddle up the pretence and reality. The day after Hope's wedding, the pretending would be over and she would have no real reason to see Max again. At that point she would need to be thinking about her own future — and that wasn't going to be in Combe St Philip or with Max.

★　★　★

After a week of rain, the sunlight struggling weakly through the clouds on Saturday made Flora restless. The cottage felt cramped after the manor, and Sweetie's incessant yowling had set her teeth on edge. Pulling on her boots, and shrugging into her coat, she set off with no clear idea of where she was going other than getting out.

Perhaps, if she walked fast enough, she could leave behind the memories of Max kissing her.

Of kissing him.

Enough! She wasn't supposed to be thinking about Max at all. They had agreed what a very bad idea it would be to get involved, and it was. Flora shoved her hands in her coat pockets and strode down the lane, into the street that curved down to the Three Bells and the centre of the village, but she had only reached the green when she heard her name being called.

'Flora! Flora!'

Puzzled, she stopped and looked around. A muddy Range Rover had pulled over on the verge near the church, and she could see Holly waving from the back seat. Ben was in the front passenger seat, his window wound down so that Max could lean across him to call her.

Her entrails promptly tied themselves into a hard knot, and her heart did a weird kind of somersault, but from somewhere she found a smile as she went over.

'Hello,' she greeted the children, flashing the smile to include Max and show that she wasn't the slightest bit awkward about seeing him. Absolutely not. 'What have you been doing?'

'We've been up to West Woods,' Ben told her. 'It was *really* muddy.'

Flora peered over the back seat to where the dogs panted happily. They were both filthy. 'So I see.'

'It's a bit of luck seeing you,' said Max, putting on the handbrake and switching off the engine. 'I had a phone call from Hope while we were out.' He nodded at the mobile phone on the dashboard.

'Is everything okay?'

'As far as I can tell. It turns out some Count — Fredrik something — is coming over from San Michele next week. He's head of security at the palace there. Presumably he's coming to check out the security situation here and liaise with the local police. Hope might want to keep it a simple wedding, but once magazines like *Celebrity* get a whiff of it, it'll be chaos down here.'

'That's true,' said Flora. 'At least the Three Bells should get some good business out of the wedding with all those paparazzi propping up the bar.'

'I assumed that this Fredrik would be staying there, but Hope's asked if we can put him up at Hasebury Hall.'

Flora turned up her collar against a sharp wind that swirled out of nowhere. 'We?'

'We're a couple, remember?'

'You said you'd be Dad's girlfriend,'

Holly piped up from the back seat.

Flora felt the colour warming her cheeks and hoped they would put it down to the cold. 'Only in San Michele and for the wedding.'

'The thing is, this Count Fredrik is part of the court, and presumably if he's head of security, it won't take him long to suss out the situation,' said Max across Ben. 'If we're pretending to be a couple for the Crown Princess, we might as well see it through.'

'Also Dad's panicking about what to give him for dinner,' Holly explained, smiling innocently when Max turned and scowled at her.

'Ah, now I see where I come in!' Flora nodded sagely. 'How long is the Count staying?'

'I'm not sure. Two or three nights? I can't give him spaghetti bolognaise every evening.'

Well, what could she say? 'I expect I could manage to cook him a decent meal. When is he coming?'

'Tuesday evening. Thanks, Flora,'

said Max gratefully.

'I don't mind. It'll be fun to meet a real-life Count. We can ask him about San Michele and how to address all those royals.'

And maybe with a third person there, the air wouldn't be jangling with memories of the feel of Max's mouth and the touch of Max's hands and the taste of Max's lips.

* * *

'I really am grateful to you for doing this,' said Max the following Monday morning. Flora was sitting at the kitchen table, drawing up a menu for the Count's visit.

'It's fine,' she said. 'It'll give me a chance to trial a few menu options for the wedding.' She put down her pen and sat back in the chair. 'I hadn't really thought about what's involved until now. I've just been focusing on the food, but that'll be the easy part. Every wedding has food. But this is a *royal* wedding, and it's going to be a logistical nightmare, isn't it? Where are all those royals going to stay, for a start? They can't all be checking into the Three Bells. They're not staying here, are they?'

Max blanched at the suggestion. 'No, thank God. I gather there's some connection with the family at Weston-bury Court, so the royal family will be staying there; but Hope will be here, plus any other bridesmaids and other hangers-on.'

'It must be a headache for the San Michele security people, having the wedding here,' said Flora, who had gone back to doodling absently.

'That's why Hope has had to fight so hard for the wedding she wants,' said Max. 'It's made her unpopular with the royal family. I think she's hoping that by offering Fredrik hospitality here, it'll show that she's not just being difficult.'

He hesitated, running a finger around his collar. 'I was wondering what you thought of the idea of moving in while

Fredrik is here?' he said, and Flora's pen skidded on the notebook.

'Moving in?' she repeated cautiously.

'I thought it might make the situation more . . . convincing,' he said. 'You'd have your own room, naturally,' he went on. 'I don't think Count Fredrik is going to be prowling the corridors to check whether we're sleeping together or not.'

'Probably not.' Flora heard a glum note in her voice, and caught herself up.

Hold on, wasn't she supposed to be feeling relieved, not disappointed?

'I'm sure that'll be fine,' she said briskly. 'We can do a practice run pretending to be a couple. It's not going to be a problem.'

★　★　★

'Ally, where are you?'

'Outside the church.'

'What on earth are you doing there at this time of the morning?' asked Flora, momentarily diverted. 'Oh, never mind,' she said before Ally could answer. 'I need you!'

Phone clamped to her ear, she was pacing up and down the bedroom Max had showed her into the day before. The décor was tired, but with fresh wallpaper and a lick of paint it could be a lovely room, with its odd angles and quirky fireplace. Like the rest of the manor now, it was sparsely furnished, but there was an inviting window seat from which you could look through the mullioned window to the walled garden below.

'Now? I'm a bit busy today,' Ally began, but Flora was not in the mood to accept any excuses.

'Today isn't the problem. It's *tonight*. You've got to help me, Ally! We've got this Count from San Michele staying here.'

'So? You were expecting him, weren't you?'

'How did you know? Sorry. I keep forgetting you're doing PR for Hope,' she said, answering her own question.

'You know much more about what's going on than I do. Anyway, Hope asked if Max would put Fredrik up, and as we're supposedly a couple, I'm staying here and playing hostess and . . . Stop laughing! It's really awkward!'

The awkwardness was with Max, but Flora didn't want to go into that.

'I can imagine,' said Ally, making what sounded like only a token effort to treat the situation with the seriousness it deserved. 'Okay, Floradear. What's the man done to get you in such a state?'

'Nothing. He's just a bit intimidating. I mean, he's perfectly polite, but he's so cool. He's got that whole sexy Special Forces thing going on — you know, all strong and silent — which is all very well until you're trying to have a conversation. Max isn't Mr Chatty either, and the arrival of the stony-faced Count poking around every corner of the Hall looking for trouble has brought home the reality of what this wedding is going to involve. It was left to me to do all the talking last night, and I was exhausted by the time I went to bed,' she remembered glumly.

'By yourself? Or did you have to be totally convincing? You know . . . with sound effects?'

'For goodness' sake, Ally! It's just a bit of play-acting,' Flora snapped before she could help herself. But honestly, it wasn't funny!'

'Sorry,' said Ally, contrite. 'To be honest, I'm having a bit of a weird one myself,' she admitted. 'Your Count caught me in full skivvy mode at the Three Bells this morning. Not exactly the impression I was hoping to make.'

'You've met him already? Well, that's perfect! You can come to dinner tonight and use your famous charm to keep things ticking over while I'm in the kitchen doing my best to convince him that we're not going to put on a hog roast to feed our royal guests.'

'I'm not sure he's impressed by my charm,' Ally said. 'He's pretty much accused me of encouraging Hope to marry her Prince in order to further my own ends.'

'Oh, for heaven's sake.'

'I know, but he's done a background check, Flora, and it was inevitable he'd think the worst. Don't worry. Once he's been softened up by your wonderful cooking it'll be a piece of cake to convince him that I'm not a wolf in rubber gloves and a pinny. I just hope Max is properly grateful for everything you're doing?'

'Not so you'd notice,' said Flora. 'I'd wittered on all evening, and I'm sure Fredrik thought I was a complete airhead; but when I said that to Max, instead of saying of *course* I didn't come over as too silly for words and thanking me for doing all the work, all he said was that he wouldn't be surprised at all,' she remembered, aggrieved.

'And he looks so sensible. He was lucky you didn't crown him with a copper-bottomed saucepan.'

'There's still time. We've got to

entertain the Count again tonight, so you've got to come and help, Ally. If nothing else, we can talk to each other.'

'Poor Floradear,' said Ally, amused. 'What's on the menu?'

'Chicken, quince and hazelnut ravioli to start, followed by roast haunch of venison with a potato and celeriac gratin, and then lemon tart,' Flora rattled off. 'What do you think?'

'Make it those pear and chocolate puddings I like instead of lemon tart, and you're on,' Ally said, and Flora cast a disapproving look into the phone.

'Chocolate will be too rich at the end of that meal.'

'Well, you *could* always chatter to Count Fredrik by yourself . . . '

Flora sighed. 'Chocolate and pear it is. Come about seven, okay? Wear something distracting.'

'I don't think Fredrik is a man to be diverted by a glimpse of gooseflesh,' said Ally, who knew how chilly Hasebury Hall could be. 'That ship sailed the minute he saw me in a headscarf and pink rubber gloves.'

'Rubbish,' said Flora stoutly. 'Do a Cinderella transformation and knock his socks off! I'll make sure Max piles the logs high in the grate.'

'Hope's the one with the Cinderella dress and glass slippers, but I'll do my best,' promised Ally. 'It should be an interesting evening.'

9

Like the rest of Hasebury Hall, the drawing room had seen better days, but Flora had drawn the heavily swagged curtains to shut out the sleety January night, and Max lit a fire in the stone fireplace. He had been left with two long, squashy sofas, but all the antique furniture that had once graced the room was gone, and there were patches on the wallpaper where valuable paintings had once hung. Flora had found some lamps to cast a yellowy glow, though, then set a line of tea-lights along the mantelpiece to add a flickering light, and it all looked cosy enough.

Count Fredrik Jensson was a tall, upright man with a steely air about him that Flora found daunting. She hadn't been at all surprised to learn that he had been a soldier. She could imagine him as a keen-eyed close protection officer, and he no doubt provided good security for the San Michele royal family, but his icy reserve was less suited to a relaxed dinner party.

Having Ally there definitely helped, though — even if it had turned out that the whole time she been talking to her friend on the phone, Fredrik had been right beside her. Flora's jaw dropped when Ally told her. 'God, he didn't hear what I was saying about him, did he? How embarrassing.'

'He didn't say anything if he did, but I don't get the impression Count Fredrik misses very much.' Ally sent their guest a cool look.

As usual, Ally looked fabulous with that not-trying-too-hard style that Flora always envied. Her outfit was sophisticated but not too formal; perfect for a winter dinner party, in fact, which was more than could be said for Flora's. She had left the kitchen long enough to run up to her room, drag a scarlet jumper over her head and pull on a pair of clean jeans. A final tousle of her hair with her fingers, a slick of bright red lipstick (*Good Time Girl*) and she was ready.

Hurrying back to the kitchen, she literally bumped into Max on the landing. He eyed her jumper dubiously.

'Don't you own anything beige?'

'Do I look like a beige person to you?'

'I just thought it would be interesting to see you in a colour that doesn't hurt my eyes.'

'I'm sorry if I don't blend with your dreary décor,' she said, 'but I'm not usually front of house. This is the warmest jumper I've got — it's cashmere, let me tell you — and I need it if I'm not going to freeze to death walking between the kitchen and the dining room.'

Max was unimpressed. 'You sound like Holly. She's always moaning about the lack of central heating. It's not *that* cold.'

'I had to get dressed under the covers

this morning. I haven't done that since I was six and my mother thought it would be a good idea to spend the winter in a tepee.'

'I'm sorry if you didn't sleep well,' said Max stiffly.

'Oh, I slept fine once I'd piled on four extra blankets,' said Flora, although that wasn't quite true. She had tossed and turned for hours, uncomfortably aware that Max was lying in bed just a couple of doors down the corridor.

Her plan not to give a moment's more thought to the way he had kissed her wasn't going well. It had been bad enough when she only really saw him in the kitchen, but persuading Fredrik that their relationship was real had meant that she could now picture him in the rest of the house too.

In spite of his shabby clothes, there was no mistaking that Max was lord of the manor. Something to do with the severe features, that autocratic nose, or the don't-give-a-damn attitude. He had a presence that came from belonging,

Flora thought. When she stood shivering next to him in the great hall to greet Fredrik, it had been easy to picture Max's ancestors looking exactly the same, striding through their hall in ruffs and embroidered doublets, in powdered wigs or mutton-chop whiskers, sublimely confident of their status as lords of all they surveyed.

It all underlined how out of place *she* was. She belonged in the kitchen, not the great hall. Flora tried not to find the thought depressing. She was certain Fredrik was going to see through the pretence. As Ally said, he didn't look as if he missed much, and it must be obvious that she was never going to be lady-of-the-manor material.

But if he had doubts, Fredrik was too polite to say so.

'I thought I would try out some possible nibbles to have at the wedding.' Flora offered round a platter of exquisitely decorated canapés, and pointed them out as Ally oohed and aahed over them. 'Smoked salmon on a beetroot blini, miniature Yorkshire puddings with rare roast beef and a horseradish mousse, and *those* are walnut sablés.'

Ally took a smoked salmon blini. 'These look fab, Floradear. How do you get them to look so pretty? They're like tiny perfect roses.'

'Do you think any of these would be suitable to serve at the reception?' Flora asked Fredrik as he took a walnut biscuit.

'I'm afraid I can't say,' he said distantly. He spoke perfect English, with a very slight, but rather sexy, accent. 'That will be for Prince Jonas and Miss Kennard to decide.'

'I don't know what's wrong with a sausage roll,' grumbled Max, but he helped himself to a Yorkshire pudding.

Flora put down the tray on the coffee table. 'If Max had his way, we'd provide the royal party with a bag of crisps and some dips,' she sighed. 'Isn't that right, darling?' she added, with a belated attempt at sounding like a real couple.

Perhaps sprinkling a few endearments around would do the trick?

'Now, now, there's no need to exaggerate, Moonflower.'

Max caught the dagger look Flora sent him at the use of her name. Served her right for 'darling'. And for turning his life upside down.

It had seemed a good idea to get Flora to the manor while Fredrik was here. Not least because he would have had to buy up Waitrose ready meals to give the man something decent to eat. And the food had been amazing. The meal she had cooked for Fredrik the previous night had been spectacular.

But now he would forever after be able to picture her everywhere: running down the stairs, hugging her arms together in the chill of the great hall, bending to add a log to the fire. He wasn't quite sure how she had done it, but a few little touches and suddenly Hasebury Hall seemed cosy and welcoming and warm, whatever she said about the lack of heating.

How was he supposed to get her out of his head now? Now that he knew how she looked curled up on his sofa, the candlelight softening the bright colours she would wear. Now that her laugh, that wickedly warm laugh that snarled his senses, lurked in every room and along the passageways. Now that her scent drifted in the air with the memory of her smile.

'Hope wants a simple wedding,' he reminded her.

Flora waved that away. 'There's simple and simple. You can have 'simple no-fuss', and 'simple exquisite', and Hope deserves the latter. I'm right, aren't I, Ally?'

'You are, you are,' Ally agreed, and Flora shot him such a triumphant look that Max could only cross his eyes at her and try not to smile.

He got up to refresh their drinks, and when he came back with the bottle, Ally and Flora were squealing with excitement about the visit to San Michele the following month.

'Omigod, Max, we're going on a private jet!' Flora was practically bouncing up and down on the sofa.

Max's brows rose. 'Oh, God, wait until Holly and Ben find that out!'

'Their Serene Highnesses, Crown Prince Carlo and Crown Princess Anna, are looking forward to welcoming you all,' Fredrik said formally. 'It will be an opportunity for the families to meet and get to know each other before the wedding in June. The Crown Prince will send the royal plane to the airport of your choice.'

'What happens once we get there?' Ally asked.

'We will, of course, issue you with a detailed itinerary nearer the time, but Prince Jonas and Miss Kennard will meet you at the airport and escort you to the palace.'

'That's in the capital, isn't it?'

'Yes, Liburno Castle. It is a very beautiful castle. I think you will enjoy your stay there.'

'Will we get a chance to see anything

of the rest of San Michele?' said Max, topping up Fredrik's glass.

'Certainly, if you wish,' said Fredrik. 'A welcome dinner has been arranged for the first night you arrive, on the Saturday, but you will have time to relax over the next couple of days, and I am sure it will be possible to show you something of the country. The engagement will be formally announced on Prince Jonas's birthday, which is on the Tuesday, and celebrated with a ball that evening.'

'A ball?' Max's heart sank. 'As in dancing?'

Flora's eyes danced as she got up to hand round the platter of canapés again. 'Of course with dancing! As in ball gowns and tiaras and an orchestra and waltzing. The real deal.'

'Oh, dear God.' Max slumped into his chair. 'Please tell me I'm not expected to dance!'

Flora laughed and perched on the arm of his chair, still holding the plate. 'Oh, but darling, you know how you love to dance with me!' she teased, resting a hand on his shoulder in a casually intimate gesture that seemed to sear through Max's shirt onto his skin.

'What's with all the darlings, *Moonflower*?' he demanded irritably in the kitchen when they were clearing away the main course, leaving Ally to earn her supper by entertaining Fredrik.

'I'm getting into part,' Flora told him with a lofty look. 'Would you rather I called you something else?'

'Yes. Max would be good.'

'Oh, but anyone can call you Max. We need a special name that demonstrates just how in love we are. Maybe you're right. Darling is a bit ordinary. Honeybun? Big Bear? Ooh, I know, what about Tiger?'

'Don't you dare!'

'Well, we need something. Fredrik certainly isn't going to get the impression we're together after the way you've been scowling at me all evening. It was like cuddling up to a block of wood earlier!' Flora picked up the gratin dish to transfer the leftovers to a bowl. 'You could at least *try* not to look as if you'd rather pick up toads than touch me with a bargepole!'

Max had had a frustrating few days. He'd been holding the carving dish with the remains of the venison, but now he plonked it down on the table, took the gratin dish from Flora's hands and put that down too, and then he kissed her, a furious kiss that snapped the tight band of tension that had had him in its grip and plunged him into a glittery maelstrom of desire. For a few moments, he lost his footing completely and spun helplessly in the scent of her and the feel of her and the warmth of her before he managed, somehow, to pull back, his breath short and ragged.

They stared at each other for long seconds until Max swore and dragged a hand through his hair.

'I don't even mind toads,' he told her, and stalked out.

Trembling with reaction, Flora set the individual chocolate and pear puddings on plates and poured cream into a jug. What had *that* been about? Max had no business kissing her like that, as if he hated her, and then walking out before she had a chance to kiss him the same way.

Flora thought she had succeeded in composing her expression by the time she took the puddings through to the dining room. Max and Fredrik were having a discussion about the economic outlook, but Ally took one look at Flora's face and mouthed *What?*.

Nothing, Flora mouthed back.

Ally's silence was eloquent with disbelief, and Flora avoided her gaze as she handed out the pudding.

'That was absolutely delicious,' Ally said, scraping the last of the chocolate out of her ramekin. 'I'll help you clear, Floradear,' she added firmly. 'Coffee, anyone?'

'What's going on between you and Max?' she asked Flora when they were safely in the kitchen.

'Nothing.'

'And why does he call you Moon-flower?'

'Private joke,' said Flora, feeling hunted. She grabbed the ramekins from Ally and dumped them in the sink to run water into them.

'Max kissed you, didn't he, when you were out here before?'

Flora gaped at Ally. 'No! He . . . How could you tell?'

'He had a muscle twitching, just here.' Ally pointed at her own jaw to demonstrate. 'I did wonder if you'd had a row, but then you came in, looking as if you'd been knocked for six, so that was a dead giveaway.'

Great. She was completely transparent.

'Honestly, it doesn't mean anything.'

Ally pointed a finger at her, not believing a word of it. 'I knew it! You and Max!'

'There isn't any me and Max.' Flora was rinsing dishes, banging them around in the sink. 'I've told you, we're pretending.'

'That is amazing.' Ally leant against the worktop, grinning. 'I had no idea you were such a brilliant actor, Floradear.'

'Aren't you supposed to be making coffee?'

'Max, too. You should both get Oscars. It's so clever the way you look at him when he's not looking at you, and he does the same thing. It's almost like you're not trying. And then you squabble like a real couple but at the same time you can practically feel the heat coming off you.'

'What rubbish,' said Flora weakly.

But Ally was on a roll. 'What's really incredible is the way you and Max have managed to get that pretend zing in the air between you. I didn't want to lean across you for the wine in case I got caught in the sizzle!'

'If we're going to talk about sizzle, what about you and Fredrik?' Flora fought back.

'Uh-uh, no changing the subject,' said Ally. 'Are you or are you not sleeping with Max Kennard?'

'No!'

'Why not?'

'Ally!'

'I'm serious. You're both single; you're both attractive, healthy adults; and please don't try telling me you don't fancy him rotten, Floradear. Why wouldn't you?'

'Because we've got nothing in common.' Flora gave in with a sigh at last. 'Because Max is always going to be bound up with his kids and his ex-wife, and I am so over pining for men who when it comes down to it are just not available. You remember what it was like with Sam, and then Rich was only available if I fitted in with his plans. Just once, I'd like to meet a guy who put me first.' She put up her chin. 'You're the one who told me I should look after myself, and that's what I'm doing. And *that's* why I'm not going to sleep with Max, okay?'

★ ★ ★

Flora shivered as she made her way along the corridor to her bedroom.

Fredrik had walked Ally home — there was definitely something going on between those two, although what exactly that something was, Flora couldn't decide — and had then retired to his room. Max had offered to help her clear up while Fredrik was out, but Flora had been so excruciatingly aware of him after that kiss that she had refused, claiming to prefer to do it by herself so that she knew where everything was. In the end, he had taken the dogs out for a walk, put his head round the door to wish her goodnight and then disappeared, presumably to bed. Without her.

Which was exactly what she wanted, Flora reminded herself. But she couldn't stop thinking about what Ally had said. *You're both single; you're both attractive, healthy adults. Why not?*

Because she was sick of taking second place, of making do with whatever was left after a glittering career or ex or children took up all the attention. Flora knew that she was right. It would be stupid to get involved with someone for whom she could only ever be second-best. She was being sensible.

So why didn't it make her feel better to be heading to a cold and lonely bed?

Pushing open her bedroom door, Flora stopped dead as blissful warmth engulfed her. For a moment she thought her senses were tricking her, but no ... An old-fashioned electric radiator stood in the middle of the room, turned up to full blast, while the bedside lamp cast an inviting glow over the bed, where a thick duvet had been laid over the one she had used the night before.

Wonderingly, Flora went over to the bed. The duvet cover was a masculine grey check, crumpled but clearly clean. Max's.

Then she saw the note tucked under the lamp. *Sorry you were cold last night. Hope you'll be able to sleep now. Thanks for the meal. M.*

As notes went, it was not exactly lover-like, but ridiculously tears pricked Flora's eyes. What was it she had said to Ally? *I'd like to meet a guy who'd put me first.* And now Max had relaxed his strict heating rule, just for her. He wanted her to be able to sleep. The thought made her feel nearly as warm as the radiator that was still blasting out heat.

Flora turned it off before she climbed into bed. Snuggling under the duvet, she was sure it held the elusive but distinctive scent of Max, and she fell asleep smiling.

★　★　★

'Thank you for the heater,' Flora said almost shyly the next morning.

'I'm sick of you complaining about the cold.' Max was at his most gruff, but then he relented. 'Did you sleep better?'

'I did. It was lovely and warm. That extra duvet made all the difference, too.

I hope you didn't give up your own?'

'I'm quite happy with a thinner one,' said Max, which Flora took to mean that it *had* been his, and the warm feeling inside her grew.

There was a tiny pause, and she wondered for one heart-pounding moment if he was going to mention that kiss, but in the end he just said, 'You deserved a decent night's sleep. You worked hard last night. Fredrik's bound to take back good reports to San Michele.'

'Well, thank you,' she said again. 'It was really kind of you.'

'Don't you dare tell Holly,' said Max, sounding more himself. 'I've spent ages arguing about heating bills with her. If she finds out that I gave you a radiator, I'll never hear the end of it.'

Now Flora didn't know *what* to think. She wondered if things might change between them after that . . . but once Fredrik had gone, she moved back to the cottage, and they carried on exactly as they had done before he had kissed her so furiously in the kitchen.

Everything was the same.

Except it didn't feel the same. That might have been because Ally was around more. Max had given her a room in the manor so that she could prepare the PR for Hope's wedding in secret before the big announcement, and she often popped in and out. Which was great, except when Max was there too and Ally would give Flora one of those knowing looks that always left Flora flustered.

She hadn't told Ally about the radiator Max had dragged into her room the night of the dinner with Fredrik. She wasn't sure why. It wasn't as if there was anything embarrassing about it. Ensuring your guests didn't freeze to death was just good manners, Flora told herself. But still, the memory felt curiously intimate, and she hugged it to herself.

Of course, one thoughtful gesture didn't change the fact that there were plenty of reasons why getting involved with Max would be a bad idea. Not least of which was the fact that he never gave any indication that he remembered kissing her at all.

Flora told herself that was just as well. She was perfectly happy to concentrate on cooking. If the evenings alone in the cottage with Sweetie felt somehow lonelier than they had done before, Flora used the time to pore over her recipes and tasting notes. She produced a selection of menu suggestions for the wedding dinner and sent them to Hope. *We can discuss in San Michele??* she put in her covering email.

The prospect of a visit to San Michele grew more and more alluring as the rain seeped unremittingly onto the bedraggled countryside. Informed that they would be travelling in the royal jet, Holly and Ben were beside themselves with excitement and could talk of nothing else over supper on Thursdays. Flora couldn't now remember when she had started eating with them. It had just seemed to happen, and had instantly become part of the weekly routine. She enjoyed both children's company; and if it was a chance to see Max without the awkwardness that inevitably slipped in when they were alone — well, she was allowed to enjoy that too.

The palace in San Michele sent them a dauntingly detailed dossier on protocol, full of instructions on what they should and shouldn't do and say, together with a more detailed itinerary. Holly cross-examined Flora on her wardrobe for each event in such detail that Flora was forced to admit that she didn't have a long evening dress.

'But there's going to be a ball!' Holly cried. 'You've got to have a ball gown!'

The upshot was an eye-wateringly extravagant shopping trip to Bath, where Flora not only bought a real ball gown in a, for her, surprisingly demure midnight blue, but also a swathe of dresses, skirts, shorts and tops, in gorgeous Mediterranean colours that she would probably never wear again, because how often, frankly, did you get invited to stay in a palace, let alone one with a sunny climate and a sparkling blue sea? If nothing else, they would be a change from the jeans, T-shirts and jumpers that were her staple wardrobe at the moment, Flora told herself philosophically. And who knew? Maybe they would get a decent summer for once and she would get more use out of them after all.

She couldn't imagine ever wearing the ball gown again, but as soon as she'd tried it on, she'd had to have it. There was a fabulous sheen to the stiffened silk that fell from the fitted bodice, and although she would normally have chosen a brighter colour, the sales assistant had persuaded her that the blue brought out the colour of her eyes and was both sophisticated and sexy.

And when Flora tried it on, she *felt* sophisticated and sexy. How could she resist? She handed over her credit card with barely a wince.

Dense fog muffled the countryside as Max drove Flora and the children to the airport in Bristol where the royal jet would be waiting for them. The blankness made his eyes ache, and it was hard to believe that the sun was still shining somewhere above it.

Fortunately, visibility had cleared by the time they got to the airport. They parked in a long-stay car park and waited for the bus to the terminal just like any other travellers, although few of those had ball gowns in carriers over their arms like Flora, but no sooner had they mentioned their names as instructed than they stepped into a different world. No queuing for check-in, just a cursory inspection of their passports and they were waved through to a vehicle that took them out to a sleek jet, discreetly painted with the arms of the royal family of San Michele.

'Wow,' said Flora as they climbed on board. Plush leather seats, real oak trims, that indefinable smell of luxury. Even Max had to admit that he was impressed. 'This is more like it.'

Ally was already on board, chatting to one of the flight attendants. She looked stylish and attractive in a grey pinstripe trouser suit with a vivid pink shirt that even Max could see was sophisticated and glamorous; unlike Flora, who was in jeans and a turquoise fleece.

'What happened to the new look?' he asked her.

'I'm waiting to surprise you. And also for it to be warmer,' she added.

Max sank into his seat and wondered what the next few days would bring. Whatever, it would be out of his hands, he told himself. He should try and relax. And as the plane nosed its way upwards through the fog and clouds and burst into the bright blue, his spirits lifted.

Behind him he could hear his children chattering, united for once in their excitement and the thrill of being invited up to the cockpit. Across the aisle, Flora and Ally had their heads together over a glass of champagne. They talked the whole way; did women never run out of conversation? Max wondered. What was so endlessly interesting, so amusing? Flora's laugh, almost but not quite dirty, drifted across the aisle. Max tried not to notice, but it was irresistible, like a warm kiss pressed against the back of his neck, making him shiver.

Except he wasn't supposed to be thinking about kisses. He had been out of line that night Fredrik came to stay, Max knew that, and warming Flora's room for her had been the least he could do to make amends. Although if the truth were known, he hadn't liked the idea of her being cold in bed. She'd needed warmth and comfort, especially after working so hard. As far as he could see, Flora looked after everyone but herself.

Not that he had any intention of looking after her, Max hastened to reassure himself. He had just been doing his duty as a host, and that included not kissing her any more. So he had done his best to keep his distance from Flora since then, but now here they were, on their way to San Michele, and they would have to spend the next five days together, pretending to be a couple. It wasn't going to be so easy to keep his distance then. Whose mad idea had that been?

Max had a nasty feeling it was his own.

'Ooh, look!' Flora pointed eagerly past him as the plane banked over the sea. Below, the Mediterranean flashed and glittered in the sunlight, and Max could make out fishing boats and cruisers far below. 'It's beautiful, isn't it?' she said, and she smiled at him, such an uncomplicated, sunny smile that he felt something unlock inside him.

He looked down at the quaint huddle of houses around the port, with the mountains rising in the distance, then back at Flora, with her blue, blue eyes and her creamy skin and the warmth that was so much part of her. He nodded. 'Yes,' he agreed.

10

Hope was waiting for them on the tarmac at Liburno airport, looking effortlessly stylish, one hand holding back her mane of wild red hair as the plane taxied towards her. Prince Jonas stood beside her, and two close protection officers lurked watchfully, expressionless behind their sunglasses. At the bottom of the steps, two sleek limousines waited, the royal flag of San Michele fluttering from their bonnets in the breeze. The sky was a bright, bright blue, and through the window Max could see palm trees rustling outside the neat terminal building.

'Now I can take my fleece off!' Flora pulled it over her head to reveal a plain white T-shirt. Casting the fleece aside, she fluffed up her hair. 'What?' she said, as she caught Max staring at her.

'Nothing.' He cleared his throat. It

wasn't so much what she was wearing as the exuberance with which she wore it. 'You're wearing white.' He was oddly disconcerted not to see her in a garish colour. 'That's practically beige.'

'I told you I had a new look,' she said; and then, when he lifted his brows, 'I'm joking. A white T-shirt isn't it. And I've still got some colour.' She stuck out her foot and twisted it from side to side so that he could admire her purple sandals and shocking pink nail polish. 'I don't want to spoil the surprise,' she told him, 'but you should see a whole new me later.'

Max felt as if he was seeing a whole new Flora already. She was usually enveloped in an apron, or in some baggy jumper, and seeing her with just jeans and a simple T-shirt was a revelation. How come he had never realized how long her legs were before? He had registered her figure before, of course he had, but now the T-shirt clung to it in a way that was quite new.

And very disturbing.

Hope was smiling as they trooped down the steps, and then they were swept into hugs and kisses and squeals of welcome. Flora liked Prince Jonas. He seemed unassuming at first sight, but he had a devastatingly attractive smile, and his eyes when they rested on Hope told Flora everything she wanted to know.

It was decided that Hope and Jonas would take Ally in their car, and that Max, Flora and the two children would follow in the second luxurious limousine. It wound its way slowly through the narrow streets of Liburno, past tall painted buildings with arched colonnades to keep the sun off the pavements. Flora glimpsed little squares with fountains, and exotic-looking churches, and then they were driving past the marina where the reflections of the elegant yachts shimmered in the water before turning back into the city.

The tyres rumbled over the cobbles of the city centre, and there were cheers and waves as pedestrians stopped to watch their prince pass. No news of the engagement had leaked out yet — Fredrik must have the security sewn up tight — but the people of San Michele must surely have been wondering about the striking redhead by Prince Jonas's side.

'Omigod,' Holly kept saying. 'This is so, so cool!' She waved out of the window with aplomb while Ben fiddled with buttons.

'For God's sake don't break anything,' Max muttered out of the corner of his mouth.

'I know, I hardly dare move,' said Flora. It had been bad enough in the plane, but now they were in this luxurious car with people staring and waving, she felt horribly out of place in her T-shirt and jeans. Why hadn't she thought more about what to wear?

'Look!' Holly pointed excitedly. 'That must be the castle!'

Looking like something out of a fairy tale with its turrets and towers, the palace seemed to grow out of a great rocky outcrop. Red-tiled houses clung to the foot of the hill, but the castle soared above them all. The road wound round the hill, climbing higher and higher until they drove through an imposing gateway to smart salutes from soldiers on either side.

The cars pulled up in a large courtyard, and there were liveried footmen to open doors and usher them up steps into the cool of the palace. Flora caught Max's eye and thought about locking the door of the cottage that morning. 'This is unreal,' she said. 'I keep thinking I'll wake up with Sweetie sitting on me, demanding his breakfast.'

Inside, the palace was opulent and hushed. Holly and Ben would be staying in the royal children's apartments, Hope told Max. 'It'll be much more fun for them.' And indeed, his children went off very happily with a capable-looking nanny, while he, Flora and Ally followed Hope up an extravagant staircase and along a bewildering labyrinth of corridors lined with paintings and sculptures and the occasional spindly table topped with some priceless piece of porcelain.

'This place makes the manor seem positively cosy,' Flora whispered to Max out of the corner of her mouth. 'I'm feeling quite homesick.'

They reached Ally's room first. Hope paused to talk to Ally, and asked a footman standing stolidly in the corridor to show Max and Flora where they would be staying. 'I'll come and find you later,' she promised them. So they followed the footman down the corridor and around a corner until he opened a door into an ornately decorated room with a spectacular view out over the city to the sea in the distance.

'For me?' Flora asked, and he smiled and gestured her into the room.

And then he gestured Max into the room too.

Murmuring something about their luggage being brought up, he withdrew.

'It looks as if we're going to be sharing,' said Max dryly.

'Oh.' Flora looked at the bed. It was an impressive piece of furniture with a high wooden frame draped in muslin, and it had a wide, inviting mattress. A mattress with nothing to stop you rolling over in the night and coming up against a lean, hard body, say.

Nothing to stop you slipping an arm over him and pressing against his back. Or kissing his neck until you made him smile and roll over and pin you into the mattress.

'Oh,' she said again. 'What are we going to do?'

Before Max could answer, there was a tap on the door, and Hope let herself in. 'You got here — good. I hear Ben's getting on like a house on fire with Mads and Cas,' she said. 'And Katja is only four and very ready to adore Holly, so I think the kids will be fine. Don't worry about them at all.'

'I'm not worrying about the *kids*,' said Max. 'I'm more worried about how

Flora and I are going to manage this week.'

'Oh, the bed,' said Hope, following his gaze. 'I'm sorry about that. I didn't know how to say you weren't sleeping together. It seemed too complicated to give you separate rooms. Is it going to be a problem?' she asked anxiously.

Flora had been watching her friend. Hope's smile seemed a little brittle, she thought. Perhaps that was only to be expected with a royal engagement coming up, and family descending. Anyone's smile would be strained.

She saw Max glance around the room. Of course there was nothing useful like a comfortable sofa, just a couple of upright chairs with ornate gilding that looked as if they would be painful to sit in, let alone try to sleep on.

But there was no point in adding to Hope's pressure by making a fuss.

'Well, not for *me*,' she said. 'I'm not sure Max is up to discovering what a sex kitten I am, though,' she said, and was relieved to see Hope laugh.

Max shook his head. Like Flora, he had noticed a frenetic edge to Hope's smile. 'We'll work something out,' he told her. 'Don't worry about it. It's not a problem.'

'Oh, *thank* you! I knew I could rely on you not to give me any more hassle. Now, drinks at six-thirty sharp in what translates as the Green Drawing Room, but you've got a couple of hours to relax before you have to be presented to the royal family.'

'Sex kitten?' Max looked at Flora when Hope had flitted away.

'I was just trying to lighten the atmosphere,' said Flora. 'Hope seems a bit on edge.'

'Yes, I noticed that too.'

Flora bit her lip. 'You don't think she's having second thoughts about marrying Jonas?'

'God, I hope not after all this. Do *you* think that?'

'No-o,' she said, but she didn't sound sure. 'They seemed good together. Not that we've had much of a chance to chat. It's probably just nerves with the engagement coming up and all the fuss. Hope's never been big on fuss, has she?'

'I hope you're right.' Max sighed and ran a hand over his hair. 'As for our situation, we'll just have to get on with it. We should have expected this, in fact, but we're both grown-ups. Sharing a bed isn't the end of the world, is it?'

'No, of course not,' Flora lied. 'There's plenty of room for both of us.'

Relax, Hope had said. How was she supposed to do *that* when she had to climb into bed next to Max in a few hours' time? It might look like a big bed, but what if it had a dip in the middle? She would never be able to sleep clinging to the side of the bed. And he would be there, with his lean, solid body, temptingly close . . .

Max pulled a dry-looking journal out of his case, kicked off his shoes, pulled some pillows behind his head and made himself comfortable on the bed, clearly taking Hope at her word. Flora couldn't help eyeing him with resentment as he put on a pair of glasses and began to read. How come *he* could look so relaxed? It wasn't fair.

We're grown-ups. So why not behave like a grown-up and get over the whole sharing-a-bed issue by suggesting that they take the opportunity to sleep together? They were both single, both unattached. What would be the harm? They had kissed, and it was no use pretending that it hadn't been nice. Surely he wouldn't have kissed her if he hadn't found her a little bit attractive?

But then he had said that it would be a *very bad idea* to take things further.

Which it would be.

A discreet knock at the door announced the arrival of their luggage. Flora's battered suitcase was placed on the floor next to Max's neat cabin bag. Would they like any help unpacking? Everyone in San Michele seemed to speak effortless English.

'I'm sure we can manage, thank you,' said Flora, trying not to giggle at the idea of anyone going through her bag.

But she could at least hang up her dresses. Very aware of Max absorbed in his journal — what was so interesting about landscape design, anyway? — she pottered around, setting out her toiletries in the bathroom and putting away her T-shirts and underwear. She set her shoes neatly in the wardrobe and tucked the empty case out of sight.

It all felt horribly intimate. Out of the corner of her eye, she saw Max turn a page. The hornrimmed glasses should have been a turn-off, but somehow they weren't. Quite the opposite, in fact.

A disturbing warmth pooled in Flora's belly, and spread out to parts of her that didn't seem to have got the message about what a bad idea it would be to go over and whip that pesky journal from his hands and toss it aside. Those bits thought it would be a great idea, in fact. Because then she could wriggle closer to him and kiss that cool, firm mouth until he smiled. She could take off the glasses and let him roll her beneath him and . . . what was bad about this idea again?

Oh, yes. Max was emotionally unavailable. They had nothing in common.

Apart from the fact that they would be sharing that bed tonight.

Oh, this was ridiculous. Flora wandered over to the long window, where the shutters had been half pulled to keep out the evening sun. Pushing them right back, she gazed down at the city spread out below her, and the sea, a glittery glare in the distance. Here she was, staying in a *palace*, in this beautiful country, and she was wasting it fretting about the night to come.

'I've got an idea.' She turned from the window.

'Mmm?' Max didn't even look up from his journal.

'I think I should cuddle up to you.'

At least that got his attention. His head jerked up and he stared at her over the rim of his glasses. '*What?*'

'I know it's silly, but the truth is, I'm a bit nervous about sleeping with you tonight. I mean, not *sleeping* with you,' she corrected herself hurriedly, 'but, you know, sleeping with you.'

'I know what you mean,' said Max in a dry voice.

Relieved, Flora pressed on. 'So, I thought that it might help if we got used to being physically close but not, er, *that* close . . . and then we might be able to relax.'

'I am relaxed,' he pointed out.

'All right, *I* might be able to relax.'

'And you think cuddling me will help you relax?' Max didn't even try to disguise his scepticism.

'I don't mean literally cuddle you. I'll just sit on the bed with you, and if we, I don't know, bump arms or something, it'll be no big deal.'

'Bumping arms has never been a big turn-on for me,' said Max, 'but if it'll stop you fidgeting, I'm all for it.' He watched as Flora grabbed her iPad, toed off her sandals, and climbed onto the bed next to him before she could lose her nerve. 'Aren't you going to read?'

'I don't think I'll be able to concentrate on a book.' The bed was high, but sumptuously comfortable, and she bounced experimentally. 'This is like the bed in *The Princess and the Pea*. Can I have one of your pillows? I suppose I could Google some menu ideas,' she said as Max pulled a pillow from behind him and passed it over to her.

'Don't you ever think of anything except food?'

I think about you, she thought, but didn't say. 'Of course I do. I often spend hours on the internet reading high-powered articles on political issues of the day. Also known as watching kitten videos.'

'Kitten videos?' Max looked as if she had confessed to watching porn.

'Look at this one.' Flora clicked on one of her favourites. It showed a tabby kitten with tiny pink paws having its tummy tickled. 'Isn't that the sweetest thing you've ever seen?'

The look Max gave her was withering.

'Okay, this one. I defy you to watch this and not have your heart melted. Sweetie must have looked like this once.' A long-haired kitten that looked like nothing so much as a ball of fluff appeared on her screen, apparently on the verge of falling asleep in spite of the fact that it was on all four paws. 'Tell me you're not in love with it,' she said.

'I'm not in love with it,' he said, deadpan, and picked up his journal once more.

'In that case there's definitely something wrong with you.'

Max found his place again. 'You're a nutcase, you know that?'

'What about a puppy video?' She clicked around for something suitably schmaltzy, knowing that it would annoy him. Actually, this was fun. It felt better to be irritating him instead of feeling awkward.

She scrolled around looking for the most endearing pictures she could find — and some of them *were* pretty cute, she had to say — contenting herself with the occasional 'Awwww . . . ' or a chuckle while a little tic developed in Max's jaw.

And the odd thing was that after a while it did feel companionable to be amusing herself with Max shaking his head at her occasionally.

'You *have* to see this one,' she told him with a nudge, and Max sighed and resigned himself to a nauseatingly sentimental video of a golden retriever puppy playing with a kitten. 'Oh . . . oh, *look*! Isn't it adorable?'

'Dear God,' he said, because he knew that was what she wanted him to say, but the truth was that he had been enjoying watching her try to provoke him. She had relaxed against the pillows, and looked rumpled and disturbingly appealing as she lounged next to him, her long legs in jeans pulled up so that she could balance the iPad against her knees. The T-shirt outlined her tempting curves, and the mischievous looks she sent him under her lashes were pure provocation.

He didn't know whether to be relieved or disappointed when Flora pulled herself upright. 'Look at the time! We should start getting ready. We'd better not be late. Is it okay if I have first shower?'

'Go ahead,' said Max, glad of some time to clear his head, although once he could hear the shower running all sensible thoughts evaporated and all he could think about was what Flora would look like under the water. He imagined that lush body naked and wet, and then he thought about her climbing into bed and spending the night next to all that warmth, and he pushed up his glasses to pinch the bridge of his nose, hard.

It's not a problem. Wasn't that what he had said to Hope? Famous last words.

'I'm going to see if I can find the kids and check they're okay,' he shouted through the bathroom door. He needed to get out before he broke it down.

When he finally tracked down Holly

and Ben, they were having a wonderful time, and had made themselves right at home in the royal children's apart-ments. The boys were racketing around together and Holly was playing Queen Bee. Trailed by little Princess Katja, a wide-eyed four-year-old, Holly proudly showed him her room and the dress she planned to wear the next day.

'We're going to eat with Mads, Cas and Katja,' she told him importantly. 'They've got their own dining room.'

'Is anyone keeping an eye on you all?'

'Oh, yes, Marta's around. She's really cool, though. She doesn't treat us like babies.' She held her hand out to Katja. 'Come on, let's go and play with your dolls' house.'

Clearly unneeded, Max made his way back to the room along the endless corridors. Opening the door, he saw Flora balancing on one leg as she slipped her foot into a shoe, but she straightened as he went in, and all the blood drained from his head. For a long moment he stared at her as she stood there in a simple sleeveless dress. It was a cheery cherry red, with a deep V-neck that drew attention to her cleavage and all that warm, creamy skin. Slightly fitted at the waist, it skimmed over her hips to end in a flirty hem above her knee, showing off her legs.

Not just legs, Max corrected himself, as blood rushed back to his brain. *Stupendous* legs that went on forever, and ended in high heels that made her even taller.

Max opened his mouth and shut it again. 'You've got legs,' he said hoarsely.

'It's my new look. What do you think?'

How was he supposed to think when she was standing there on those legs? She had done something to her face, too. Max wasn't sure what, but she looked more sophisticated than usual. Sexier.

'You look . . . you look . . . ' God, listen to him stuttering like an idiot! ' . . . nice,' he managed.

He could tell by her face that *nice* was an inadequate response, but he was rattled.

'Very nice,' he tried again.

Flora rolled her eyes. 'Are you going to have a shower?'

'Yes, I think I will,' said Max. He had better make it a cold one, he added to himself.

11

'I wish I hadn't worn heels,' Flora muttered to Max as they stood looking up a magnificently curved marble staircase. 'My feet are killing me. We must have trekked miles already.'

'Come along, my little Moonflower, I think we've just got to get up these stairs.'

'Don't call me Moonflower.' But when he offered her his hand, Flora took it, glad of his warm grip as she teetered up the stairs. What had she been thinking, trying to be sophisticated? The kind of woman who wore heels? She should have known she would never be able to carry it off. So much for trying to dazzle Max, too. *Very nice* had been the best he could manage.

But his fingers did feel good wrapped around hers.

At the top of the stairs, they found themselves facing an array of footmen in ornate uniforms, two of whom stepped forward smartly to fling open the two halves of a double door. Max and Flora walked obediently through, and stopped dead, jaws dropping in unison.

They found themselves in a sumptuously decorated room. The windows were lavishly draped in swagged green silk, the walls hung with green and gold. There was an elaborately gilded plasterwork ceiling, a riot of painted gold swags and garlands decorated the cornices, and even the carpet was patterned in gold. Massive chandeliers glittered; priceless works of art decorated the walls. The effect was dazzling, if overwhelming.

Max recovered first. 'Just your ordinary family get-together,' he murmured to Flora, who was still gaping at the splendour.

At first sight, she had thought the room was crowded with strangers, and for one ghastly moment thought that they were going to be announced by a stentorian butler as if they were attending a Regency ball, but thankfully Hope was looking out for them and hurried over.

'Flora, look at you in heels! You look fabulous!'

'Now, that's how it's done,' Flora said to Max, gratefully accepting a glass of champagne from a tray.

'How what's done?' Hope asked.

'When I asked your brother if I looked okay, he just said I looked 'nice'.'

'Oh, Max, you can do better than that!' said Hope.

'I said 'very nice',' Max corrected, 'but I meant 'gorgeous'.'

There was a fizzing silence. Hope's eyes flickered between the two of them with interest. Flora felt her cheeks grow pink. She took a slug of champagne. 'Well, that's a bit better,' she said.

'You really do,' he said.

'You're being nice,' she said, more

unsettled than she wanted to admit; and, trying to make a joke out of it, 'Who are you, and what have you done with Max?'

'Looks like you can't win, Max,' said Hope. 'Come and be presented to the Crown Prince and Princess,' she went on, tucking her hand into his arm. 'They're hosting all the events this week as Jonas's father is still convalescing.'

'Is this Anna, the Crown Princess with the obsession about protocol?' Max lowered his voice as Hope led them across the room.

'That's the one.' Hope's smile was suspiciously brittle. 'Actually, she's all right when you get to know her. Carlo can be a bit stiff, but he's decent.'

'Do we have to curtsey or anything?' Flora asked nervously.

'It's just an informal affair tonight, but Anna would probably like it if you could manage a quick bob, anyway.'

Flora glanced around the room with its gilt and gold and glittering chandeliers. Informal. Right.

Hope led them over to a haughty-looking couple. Anna, the Crown Princess, was cool and blonde and immaculately groomed, her hair smoothed and twisted into a sophisticated chignon. She was very slim. Between her and Hope and what looked like every other woman in the room, Flora felt like a water buffalo who had strayed into a crowd of gazelles.

Why, oh why, had she worn heels? Keeping hold of her champagne, she managed a sketchy curtsey, which the Crown Princess acknowledged with a dip of her head, but getting up proved to be harder than getting down, especially on her heels. Flora wobbled perilously as she tried to straighten and for an endless horrified moment thought she was going to topple over completely. Just in time, a firm hand gripped her elbow and pulled her upright. Max. Torn between gratitude and giggles at how nearly she had fallen splat in front of the Crown Princess, she smiled at him. *Thank you*, she mouthed.

Max just looked pained.

After the initial presentation, Hope murmured an excuse, and Max and Flora were left to make laboured conversation with the Crown Prince and Princess. The advice they had been sent by the protocol department had instructed that they were not to ask direct questions, which made small talk tricky. Max seemed to be getting on okay with the Crown Prince, but Crown Princess Anna was harder work. Flora gulped her champagne and agreed that they had had an easy trip and that their room was very comfortable.

'Have you and Max known each other long?' Anna beckoned over a footman with a tray and indicated that Flora's glass was empty.

'You could say that. I had a crush on him when I was fifteen,' said Flora as she exchanged her empty glass for a full one.

'Ah, you were childhood sweethearts?'

'Not exactly. I'm quite sure Max

didn't know I existed then,' Flora said, taking a fortifying slug of champagne.

'So you have met again recently?'

'Yes, just last year, in fact.' Anna had an expression of polite interest fixed on her face, but showed no inclination to talk about her own relationship, which left Flora to burble on. 'We've been spending a lot of time together.' Which was true, after all. 'And you know how you can know someone for ages, and then quite suddenly you look at them, and bam! That's it. He's the one, I said to myself.'

Her heart squeezed queerly and she found her eyes resting on Max's profile as he nodded at something Prince Carlo was saying. *He's the one.*

'You are lucky to have found each other.' Anna sounded almost wistful.

Flora jerked her gaze from Max's mouth. 'I know.'

'It seems love is in the air, what with Jonas and Hope's engagement, and now you and Max. Will you be getting married too?'

Well, why not? If she was going to pretend, she might as well do it properly, right? She nodded with what she hoped was a suitably besotted smile. 'When you've found the right one, why wait?'

'Hope didn't mention that her brother was engaged.'

Flora could see Anna trying to work out if there were any implications for protocol. 'We haven't made it official yet,' she said, before Anna could comment on the lack of a stonking diamond on her finger. 'We don't want to take attention from Hope and Jonas.'

'That is very thoughtful of you.' The Crown Princess smiled thinly. 'Congratulations. I wish you every happiness.'

'Thank you.' Flora took another swig of champagne, thinking that she had brushed through the interrogation pretty well, until the Crown Prince, who must have had ears like a bat, turned to them. 'Did I hear congratulations are in order?'

'Max and Flora are engaged,' Anna told him. 'They're keeping the news quiet until after Jonas and Hope's engagement is announced at the ball on Tuesday.'

Flora risked a glance at Max's rigid face. Moving closer, she tucked her hand into the crook of his arm and smiled winsomely, or so she hoped. 'Don't be cross with me, darling,' she said to him. 'I know we agreed to keep it a secret, but I couldn't help it.' She opened her eyes wide, playing the ditzy blonde for all she was worth. 'It's just too hard to keep our happiness to myself.'

Max glanced at the Crown Prince and Princess, who were watching with interest. A muscle was hammering in his jaw, and Flora could see the effort it cost him to unclench his teeth.

'We'd be glad if you wouldn't pass on the news just yet,' he said, with a repressive look in Flora's direction. 'This is Hope's time.'

'Oh yes, of course, we understand. But our felicitations.'

Max took Flora by the arm and

practically dragged her away. 'Since when have we been engaged?' he demanded furiously out of the corner of his mouth.

'Since we fell so madly in love,' said Flora, slightly giddy from a mixture of nerves and champagne. 'Surely you remember?'

'*Flora* . . . ' he ground out, and she held up her hands, one still clutching her glass, in surrender.

'I'm sorry, I'm sorry! I was nervous, okay?'

'Nervous?' Max was propelling her through the crowded room, clearly determined to get her as far away from the Crown Prince and Princess as possible. 'What have you got to be nervous about?'

About lying next to you in bed. About keeping my hands off you. About pretending that I love you while pretending that I don't want you to kiss me again.

'I'm not used to meeting royalty,' she blustered instead. 'I was trying to remember everything they said on that protocol document they sent out, and it just kind of . . . slipped out.'

'Well, please don't let anything else *slip out*,' said Max.

'Oh, it's not that bad,' said Flora. 'It's not as if they're going to tell anyone. For a start, they're not going to be interested in us; and anyway, Anna doesn't seem the gossipy type.'

'I hope to God you're right,' he said morosely.

'Honestly, Max, anyone would think you didn't want to marry me.'

Another footman in breeches and a gorgeously frogged coat paused by them and offered a tray of food.

'Ooh, look at those canapés!' Flora studied them with professional interest. 'Aren't they pretty?' She took one with a smile of thanks and popped it in her mouth. 'Mmm, delicious! Try one of those, Max.'

He cast her a resigned look, but obeyed.

'What do you think?' she asked as he

chewed. 'Are you getting a touch of fennel in the pastry?'

'No idea,' he said unhelpfully.

'I should go and talk to the palace chef while I'm here. I mustn't forget that I've got a wedding to cater!'

'You seem to have forgotten everything else we specifically agreed,' Max groused.

'We agreed we would pretend to be having a relationship,' Flora pointed out. 'I've just embellished a little bit.'

'A bit? It's a hell of a leap from girlfriend to fiancée!'

'Look, there's no need to panic. I don't really see what difference it makes, and besides, nobody needs to know about it.'

'What's this I hear about you two being secretly engaged?' Hope popped up behind them. 'I said to Ally, I *thought* there was something going on between the two of you!'

'Nothing's going on,' said Max curtly. 'Flora's just had too much champagne.'

The second glass of champagne was indeed having its effect and Flora was back in a buoyant mood. She was in a fair way to forgetting how nervous she had been feeling about sharing a bed with Max. She was even forgetting how much her feet hurt.

'I might have suggested something to Anna by mistake,' Flora conceded with a wave of her glass, 'but it isn't a big deal. We'll split up after we go home.'

'And then get engaged again for the wedding?' Max asked, exasperated.

'That's the kind of on-off relationship we have.' Flora was beginning to feel a bit tipsy. 'I'm going to dump you, by the way, Max,' she told him.

'On what grounds?'

'I'll say you can't satisfy me in bed.'

Max turned to his sister. 'I have to put up with this all the time now,' he informed her.

Hope looked from one to the other. 'You seem to be getting on okay.'

'A few weeks ago, I had a nice quiet life,' he grumbled. 'Now my sister is going to be a princess and I'm apparently engaged!'

'Ignore him, Hope,' said Flora. 'Underneath that grumpy exterior, he's thrilled really.' Encouraged by Hope's smile and the way the tense look around her eyes had eased, she went on. 'Our wedding is going to be much grander than yours, by the way. No simplicity for us! I'm going to go the full meringue on the dress front, and after the ceremony, Max is going to lift me up before him onto a white horse so we can ride back to Hasebury Hall. It's going to be so romantic, isn't it, darling?' she added with a mischievous look at Max, who shook his head at her.

'If anyone asks, we're eloping,' he said firmly.

'That sounds like a great idea,' said Hope, and the bleakness in her voice made Max frown.

'You okay, Hopey?'

Hope sighed. 'Oh, it's just . . . ' But before she could go on, she caught sight of a slim, dark-haired woman hovering, clearly waiting to speak to them. Her expression wiped clean. 'I'm fine.' She flashed a brilliant smile. 'Let me introduce Celina Harris. Celina is social secretary to Jonas's grandmother, the Dowager Princess Margaret.'

'You're American,' said Flora in surprise when Hope had made the introductions and they had all shaken hands.

'That's right,' said Celina with a pleasant smile. She was very attractive and well-groomed, discreetly dressed in subtle colours that made Flora feel clown-like in her red dress. 'I'm so sorry to interrupt you, but the Dowager Princess would very much like to meet you both. May I present you to her?'

'Good luck!' said Hope, abandoning them.

'Do we need luck?' Flora asked Celina nervously as she led them over to where an elderly but imperious-looking lady was sitting on a spindly, gilt-legged sofa.

Celina laughed. 'Don't worry! The

Dowager Princess can seem intimidating at first, but underneath, I promise you, there's a heart of gold — although she would be mad at me for saying so, I know!'

She stopped in front of the sofa. 'Your Highness, may I present Sir Max Kennard, Hope's brother, and Flora Deare, his . . . ' She looked enquiringly at Max who sighed, clearly resigning himself to the inevitable.

'My fiancée,' he supplied.

12

'Indeed!' The Dowager Princess's brows shot up. 'Hope didn't mention it.'

'Our engagement is very recent,' he said in a dry voice.

'Well, I'll talk to you later,' she said, dismissing him with a wave of her hand. To Flora's surprise, the Dowager spoke in a cut-glass English accent. San Michele seemed to be a real melting pot of nationalities. 'For now, I want to talk to this Flora.'

Discreetly, Celina led Max away. Flora cast a longing glance after them. The Dowager Princess seemed very fierce, and after three glasses of champagne — or was it four? — she wasn't sure she was up to an interrogation.

'Tall girl, aren't you?' said the Dowager with a critical look. She nodded at the space on the sofa beside her. 'Sit down. I don't want to crane my neck to talk to you.'

Flora looked doubtfully at the sofa. She hoped it would hold her weight. Very carefully she lowered herself to perch on the edge, still clutching her glass. It wasn't the kind of sofa you could loll on, and she found herself imitating the Dowager's ramrod-straight back.

'It's quite a relief to sit down,' she confided. 'I don't usually wear heels, and my feet are killing me.'

The Dowager was unsympathetic. 'Better to have sore feet than to wear the wrong shoes.'

Well, that was her put in her place, Flora thought.

'I'd rather be unfashionable,' she said frankly. 'I spend all day on my feet in the kitchen, and I have to have comfortable shoes. I'm a chef,' she explained when the Dowager lifted autocratic brows.

'Indeed? And how does a chef get to be engaged to a baronet?'

Very good question. But not for the reason the Dowager thought. Flora put up her chin. 'By falling in love,' she said.

'Hmpphh. He's divorced, I hear? People divorce too easily nowadays,' the Dowager declared. 'When I was young, we said our marriage vows and meant them. Why would you want to marry a man who's already given up on a marriage?'

'Max didn't *give up* on his marriage,' Flora fired back instantly. 'That's not fair. He's had to deal with a huge amount. I'm sure you know all about his father's scandal, but Max was the one who had to keep the family going and sort out all the debts. He's managed to hold on to his inheritance and build a business. His children are happy. If his marriage collapsed under the pressure, that's not all going to be his fault; and isn't it better to have the courage to admit that you've made a mistake than for both parties to be miserable? I say Max deserves to be happy, and if I can make him happy, then you know what? I deserve to be happy too.'

She drained her glass as she finished, defiant but obscurely depressed, too, at the knowledge that she would never be the one to make Max happy.

She half expected to be slapped down for speaking back to a princess, but the Dowager just favoured her with a hard stare before abruptly changing tack.

'What's all this nonsense about a village wedding for my grandson?'

She proceeded to cross-examine Flora on Combe St Philip and its suitability or otherwise to host a wedding for the royal house of San Michele, while Flora did her best to counter the volley of questions.

It was a huge relief when Celina materialized with another victim — *guest*, Flora corrected herself — for the Dowager to grill. Flora leapt to her feet to relinquish her seat on the sofa, not even minding being on her heels again.

'Phew!' she said, casting Celina a glance speaking of gratitude. 'She's absolutely terrifying! How on earth do you work for her?'

'She's a sweetie when you get to know her,' said Celina.

A *sweetie*? About as sweet as Sweetie

himself, Flora reckoned; which was to say, not at all.

Celina laughed at Flora's flabbergasted expression. 'She liked you — I could tell.'

'Really? I'd hate to be someone she disliked in that case. I feel like a dragon has chewed me up and spat me out!'

'Have another glass of champagne,' said Celina soothingly, beckoning over a footman. 'That'll make you feel better.'

* * *

Twenty or so people sat down for dinner around a mahogany table polished to a mirror-like shine and laden with silver and glasses that sparkled in the light of the massive chandeliers. Flora was used to elaborate place settings in the restaurant, of course, but even she was daunted by the array of cutlery, precisely set around each mat. She imagined a butler overseeing footmen with a ruler, measuring out the distance between forks to the millimetre.

Flora had been afraid she might have to endure another interrogation from the Dowager, so was relieved to find herself on the other side of the table. Max, it seemed, had drawn the short straw, and was placed next to the old lady. In spite of her earlier disparaging comments, the Dowager seemed to be enjoying his company, judging by the occasional crack of laughter. And Max was obviously finding her equally entertaining. Perhaps the Dowager Princess only snacked on young female chefs to whet her appetite for dinner?

And how come the Dowager wasn't messing up the Crown Princess's seating plans? Flora wondered owlishly, having lost count of how many glasses of champagne she had had by the time they sat down to dinner. *She* hadn't been required to bring a partner to dinner to even up the numbers.

Flora herself was sitting a little further down and across the table from the Dowager and Max, between Jonas's brother, Prince Nico, and a Count whose name she didn't catch but who was apparently some distant cousin, and who ogled her cleavage openly as he unfolded his napkin.

Nico, as he insisted she call him, waving aside his princely title, was clearly a practised charmer. It was a little overwhelming to find herself sitting next to someone whose jet-setting exploits were regularly chronicled in *Celebrity* and *Glitz*, and who was even more handsome close up than he was when shot through the lens of a paparazzo zoom.

Nico was obviously skilled at drawing out dazzled guests, though, and when he saw how carefully she tasted and analysed each dish, he forgot his flirtatious manner and Flora forgot to be overwhelmed, and they had a stimulating discussion about food and wine. Nico was flatteringly interested in Flora's plans for her own restaurant, and she soon relaxed and quite forgot that he was a prince at all.

It would have been a very enjoyable

evening if she hadn't been so uncomfortably aware of Max on the other side of the table. Flora kept missing the thread of what Nico was saying as Max bent his head towards the Dowager and his stern face would be illuminated by that rare smile of his. Every time he smiled, it snagged at the edge of her vision, which was ridiculous. It was only a smile, after all.

It was just that he never smiled at her like that, Flora thought crossly. And she was his fiancee!

Well, not really his fiancee, of course, but still.

She'd seen him smile at Celina too, and Hope, and Ally, and everyone except her, now Flora came to think of it.

Except he had said that she was gorgeous earlier. He had even sounded as if he meant it. But even if he had meant it, he had probably changed his mind after she had claimed to be engaged to him, and —

And what was *wrong* with her? Flora

wanted to slap herself. Here she was, sitting next to a real-life prince — a handsome, charming prince who was actually flirting with her — and all she could do was notice Max smiling. It was infuriating.

If only he would stop *sitting* there, and *looking* like that, and *smiling* like that, she could relax and talk to Nico. Turning determinedly back to the prince, Flora offered him a dazzling smile. She was *not* going to think about Max any more. She was going to enjoy Nico's company, and if Max realized what a good time she was having without him, so much the better.

★   ★   ★

The Dowager Princess had clearly cornered the market in indomitable old ladies and had everyone running scared of her, although personally Max liked the unmistakable glint in her eye. He enjoyed her astringent manner, which was not so different from his own, in fact, and would have been perfectly happy talking to her all night if his meal hadn't been ruined by his perfect view of Flora on the other side of the table.

He tried not to watch her. He really did. But really, it was almost seductive, the way she ate, putting a forkful in her mouth, tasting carefully, the blissful expression when she approved, or a slightly squinty-eyed assessing look as she tried to work out the combination of flavours. No wonder Prince Nico, who was sitting next to her, had a dazed look, his tongue practically hanging out of his mouth.

And as for the flirting that was going on . . . Nobody would guess that Flora was supposedly engaged to *him*, Max thought savagely. She seemed to have forgotten that she had invented *that* little story. Instead she was laughing immoderately at whatever Nico said, that husky laugh that seemed to trail teasing fingers over Max's skin and clench at the base of his spine, or leaning forward to give Nico a good view of that spectacular cleavage. If the prince wasn't careful, he would fall into it.

'There's no use glaring, young man,' said the Dowager, who had been observing him with cynical amusement. 'That'll just encourage her.'

'I beg your pardon?' he said, taken aback.

'You needn't get all hoity-toity with me,' she said. 'I may look like an old woman, but I remember what it's like to run rings round a man, and young Miss Deare over there clearly knows what she's doing too.'

Max glowered.

'If it's any comfort, it's all for your benefit,' said the Dowager.

It didn't look to Max as if Flora had any interest in him at all. That smile, that luscious display of cleavage, was clearly aimed at the man next to her. A man, Max reminded himself, who was handsome, seductive, and single — oh, and a prince, as if he wasn't nauseating enough already.

A handsome prince who was clearly just as taken with Flora as she was with him. Why wouldn't she be interested? Max reminded himself dourly. Nothing surprising about the fact that she would prefer Nico to a cranky divorced father of two.

He just wished that he wasn't aware of every time she laughed or closed her lips over a mouthful of food, of every time she turned her head. He wished he could forget about how she looked in that dress with those unexpectedly spectacular legs, or how it had felt to kiss her, that yielding warmth and sweetness that had caught him unawares.

He wished he could stop thinking about what it would be like to sleep next to her tonight.

★   ★   ★

Between Flora's flirting and the Dowager Princess's pointed questions about their supposed engagement, the meal dragged interminably, and there was still more small talk to be endured in the White Drawing Room after dinner, where they were served coffee in impossibly fragile and probably priceless porcelain cups and saucers.

As if that wasn't prolonging the agony enough, Jonas offered liqueurs. 'Don't you think you've had enough, *darling*?' Max said to Flora with a meaningful look as she clapped her hands together.

'I'll just have a little Calvados as a *digestif* to settle my stomach.' She smiled wickedly at him and something unlocked inside Max with a little sigh of warmth. Flora was swaying slightly, but her eyes were a deep blue and her mouth a warm, inviting curve and in that red dress she looked so delectable that Max began to feel dangerously giddy, almost as if he had had too much to drink too.

Almost as if he needed to gather her closer so that they could hold on to each other.

Luckily, Flora spotted Ally behind

him, declared that she needed to speak to her, and tottered off unsteadily on her heels.

'Max.'

Hope's voice at his elbow jolted him back to reality, and he turned to his sister, hoping that she hadn't seen him staring after Flora.

She had, of course. 'I like seeing you and Flora together,' she said. 'It makes me feel something good has come out of all this.'

Max had opened his mouth to deny that he and Flora were together when his brain caught up and he realized what Hope had said.

'Something good . . . ? Hopey, are you all right?' he asked in concern.

'Oh, yes, I'm just . . . ' She sighed. 'It's all a bit much, you know?'

Max followed her gaze around the drawing room with its marble fireplace, ornate plasterwork and elaborately swagged curtains. There were gold tassels by the yard, and more gilt on the groups of eighteenth-century sofas and chairs.

249

'I can imagine,' he said.

'Max,' Hope began impulsively, and then changed her mind. 'Oh, ignore me!' she said with a lightning switch of mood. 'Come and meet Nico.'

Frankly, Prince Nico was the last person Max wanted to meet, but he allowed himself to be towed across to the other side of room from Flora, who had established herself as principal entertainer, judging by the laughter around her. The Dowager Princess and the Crown Prince and Princess left early, and their departure was the sign for the party to relax — or relax even more in Flora's case, Max thought darkly.

He had exchanged a few pleasantries with Prince Nico, but was glad to be rescued after a while by Celina Harris. He approved of her neatness, her dark smooth hair, her quiet grace and elegance — unlike *some* people he could mention — but it was hard to concentrate on what she was saying when Flora's laugh was tangling up his senses and tripping up his breathing. Making him think about the way she had sprawled on the bed next to him, and how easy it would have been to roll her beneath him and get his hands on that lovely, warm, creamy skin at last.

Making him wonder if he would have another chance that night, and what he would do about it if he did.

'Flora's so fun,' Celina said. 'Is she always the life and soul of the party?'

'Pretty much,' said Max.

He watched Flora across the room as she gesticulated, her face animated, and the group around burst out laughing anew. Did she always feel like being fun? Max wondered. How much of that cheerfulness was designed to make everyone else feel better? Even at her grandfather's funeral she had made sure that she greeted everyone with a bright smile.

By the time Max made his way back to Flora's side, she was well away.

'My fiancé!' she cried in greeting and flung her arms around his neck.

Max held her in a firm grip, keeping all that lush warmth pressed against him. She smelt of rosemary, he thought inconsequentially. Like the herb garden on a warm summer evening.

'I think it's time we got you to bed,' he said dryly. 'We had an early start, and you're tired.'

He manoeuvred her out of the room and they began to descend the marble staircase. 'You'd better hold on to me,' Max told Flora.

'Well, I might,' she said, taking his arm. 'But only because I'm a bit wobbly in my heels,' she added with dignity, only to spoil the effect with a hiccup. Covering her mouth with her free hand, she peeped a glance at Max, laughter dancing in the blue, blue eyes.

'God, you're drunk,' Max sighed, but he could feel the corner of his mouth twitching in spite of himself.

At last they made it back to the room. He propped Flora up inside while he closed the door, and by the time he turned back, she had staggered over to the bed and flopped across it, face down.

Max stood looking at her for a moment, and then he went to sit on the bed by her feet so that he could pull off the frivolous shoes. Unthinkingly, he massaged the balls of her feet, and she made a sound low in her throat, like a purr; and, like a cat, she rolled luxuriously over and flung her arms above her head.

There was a roaring in Max's ears, and a dark haze in front of his eyes. Was he really expected to sit here, while Flora lay in tempting abandon, her mouth curved so invitingly? Letting go of her foot to lean over her in anticipation, Max stopped at the sound of the unmistakable whistle through her mouth. She might look seductive, but Flora was sound asleep.

* * *

When Flora woke the next morning, the inside of her skull was thumping and her tongue was stuck to the roof of her mouth. Cautiously, she prised open her eyelids, and winced at the glare. She was lying under the covers in her bra and the thong she had bought specially to wear under the red dress, which appeared to be draped over a chair she could just see out of the corner of her eye without turning her head, which seemed too risky a procedure to attempt just yet. When had she taken her dress off?

Oh, and now it seemed that she had been sleeping with her mouth open and had dribbled onto the pillow. Excellent.

Flora lay rigidly still in the hope that the thudding in her head would subside, while hideous flashes of memory jumbled around in her brain.

Drinking champagne.

Sore feet.

Telling the Crown Princess that she and Max were engaged. God, what had she been thinking?

The meal had been good; she remembered *that*. Trying to talk to Nico while Max's smile tugged at the edge of her vision.

Thinking another Calvados would be a good idea.

Clinging on to Max on the marble staircase.

But then what?

Blearily, she heard the door open and footsteps approaching the bed. 'Are you awake?' Max asked.

'Eurgghh,' was all Flora could manage.

'Not feeling well?'

'I think I might actually be dying.'

'That's what happens when you guzzle a vat of Calvados on top of a crate of champagne,' said Max unsympathetically; but he poured her a glass of water and helped her up, ignoring her yelp of pain when what felt like a cleaver split her head, so that she could sip at it. 'Here, I brought you a couple of aspirin,' he said.

'Thank you,' said Flora weakly as she collapsed back against the pillows, very conscious that she was only in her underwear. 'Um, last night . . . ? Did I undress myself?'

'You roused yourself enough to turn over so that I could unzip you, but that was as much as you could do,' Max told her. 'I had to manhandle you out of your dress. It wasn't the easiest job in the world, but it had some compensations,' he added in a dry voice, and she flushed, thinking of just how much flesh must have been on display.

'Where did you sleep?'

He nodded at the bed. 'Right next to you.'

'Oh.' Her colour deepened. 'But we didn't . . . er, you know . . . ?'

Max put on a puzzled expression. 'What?'

'*You* know . . . '

'Sorry, I'm not following,' he said, straight-faced.

Flora scowled. He was being deliberately obtuse. 'Did we *sleep* with each other or not?' she said through gritted teeth, and Max reeled back, clapping his hand to his heart and assuming — she was sure — a shocked expression.

'You mean you don't remember? The earth moved, the angels sang, stars burst overhead — '

'Very funny,' she interrupted him mirthlessly. 'Be serious, Max. What really happened?'

'Well, luckily for you, I've never been interested in unconscious ladies. It was all I could do to sleep at all with you snoring like a sailor all night.'

'Great.' It just kept getting better and better. Dribbling, all her podge revealed, and now snoring.

'It was a memorable night, I can tell you that,' he said. 'Although clearly not for you.'

'I wish I *could* remember it,' sighed Flora. 'Max, did I do anything awful? I'd hate to have embarrassed Hope.'

'I don't think Hope was embarrassed. The royal family on the other hand . . . '

'Oh God, what did I do?'

'You kicked off the evening with a bare-faced fib to the Crown Prince and Princess about us being engaged,' Max reminded her severely, and she bit her lip.

'I do remember that,' she admitted.

'And then, having engaged yourself to me, you proceeded to spend the whole night flirting with Prince Nico, and making me look a fool.'

Flora pulled a face. 'I'm sure I wasn't *flirting*. I've always been hopeless at that.'

'It looked like it from where I was sitting,' said Max. 'Even the Dowager Princess commented on it. She told me you would lead me a pretty dance. She seemed to find that amusing for some reason,' he brooded, remembering.

'What form did this flirting take?' asked Flora suspiciously.

'Oh, you know. Batting your lashes and tilting your head and giving him lots of opportunities to peer down your cleavage. Smiling at whatever he said. *Oh Nico, that's so interesting. Oh Nico, you're so handsome.*' Max put on an excruciating falsetto voice, and his imitation simper was so ridiculously exaggerated that Flora couldn't help laughing.

'I bet I wasn't that bad!'

'Not far off,' he grumbled. 'I felt an absolute fool. First prince who comes along, and my alleged fiancée ignores me completely!'

'Well, I'm very sorry,' said Flora placatingly. 'I didn't mean to embarrass you.'

'I survived.' Max relented. 'The truth is, you were good fun,' he admitted. 'You helped brush through one or two sticky moments, which would have been much more awkward if you hadn't been there keeping everyone laughing.'

Alarmed, Flora sat up, if cautiously. 'What kind of sticky moments?'

'Nothing dramatic, but I'm worried about Hope. She's not herself.'

'I remember thinking that before . . . I hope she's okay.'

'Probably pre-engagement-party jitters,' said Max. 'She should have had a vat of champagne like you, and then she'd have been fine.'

Flora looked fixedly at him. 'Are you quite sure I didn't do anything too embarrassing last night?'

'Cross my heart and hope to die,' said Max, deadpan, but a smile was lurking around his mouth in a most distracting way.

'That's a relief.' Flora seized on the excuse to close her eyes and lean back, although the almost-smile still danced behind her eyelids. 'Doesn't make my head feel any better, but it is a relief.'

'You can't have everything,' Max agreed.

A little silence fell. 'How long have you been up?' Flora asked at last, opening her eyes.

'A while. I've had breakfast with Holly and Ben. I thought I'd better tell them we're engaged now.'

Flora winced at the memory. 'What did they say?'

'Ben said 'cool', and Holly wants to be your bridesmaid too. I said I didn't think you'd mind.'

'No, of course not . . . but wait, hang

on . . . ' Flora put a hand to her aching head. 'She knows we're not really getting married, doesn't she? I mean, they know what's going on?'

'If they do, it's more than I do,' said Max.

13

'How are you feeling?' Ally was sitting on a terrace, looking as stylish as ever, her feet up on the balustrade and a notebook on her lap. She grinned as Flora lowered herself very cautiously into a chair beside her.

'Disgusting.' Flora looked at the cup and saucer on the table beside Ally. 'Where did you find the coffee?'

'Oh, my dear!' Ally put on a grandly patronizing voice. 'You don't get your own coffee. You ring a bell and someone will bring it to you.' Picking up the little bell on the table, she demonstrated; and sure enough, a discreet footman appeared and asked what Flora would like in impeccable English.

'Coffee, please, if it's not too much trouble.'

'It's a weird life, isn't it?' said Ally when he had gone. 'I mean, it's fabulous for a few days, but would you like to live like this all the time?'

'No. I'd hate someone else doing all the cooking, for a start.'

'I should interview you some time about what you're doing for the wedding. I need to get Max on what it's like to host a royal wedding, too,' she remembered. 'Where is he, anyway?'

'He's gone on some boat trip that's been organized for the kids.'

'Didn't you want to go?'

'I could hardly crawl out of bed, let alone face bobbing around on a boat.' Flora held on to her still-thumping head. Just thinking about being on a boat made her feel seasick. 'I opted to stay here and die quietly instead. I am never drinking again, by the way.'

The footman appeared with her coffee just then, and she sipped it gratefully.

'So, you and Max?' said Ally when he'd gone.

'There is no me and Max,' said Flora firmly.

'Hey, I heard you got engaged.'

'That was my fault. I got a bit carried away by the pretence, that's all.'

'I thought you looked pretty good together last night.'

'Oh, please.'

'You must have thought about it.'

'Well, maybe once or twice,' Flora conceded, 'but that lord-of-the-manor thing doesn't really do it for me.' *Liar*, she thought. 'And anyway, he's not available.'

'Sure he is. He's divorced.'

'He's not *emotionally* available. Nothing's changed from when we talked about this before, Ally. Stella's always ringing him up and checking on him, and he never tells her to leave him alone.'

'They're probably talking about Holly or Ben — and by the way, when did you get to be so good with children? I watched you on the plane. You're great with them, and they obviously love you.'

Flora shifted uncomfortably. 'They're kids. They love everyone.'

'You can't hold talking to Stella against Max, Floradear. She's always going to be Holly and Ben's mother. She's part of the package, and surely it's better that they get on instead of fighting the whole time, which is what a lot of divorced parents I know do. That's what happens if you get involved with a divorced guy if he's got kids.'

'Yes, well, that's why I'm *not* getting involved,' said Flora, pushing the memory of that kiss firmly aside. 'It would never work, even if either of us did want to get involved, which we don't. Max is wedded to Hasebury Hall. That's his life and he's never going to leave it, and I'm going back to London just as soon as I can sell the cottage after the wedding.'

'The wedding's not until June,' said Ally, flipping her notebook closed and getting to her feet. She smiled down at Flora. 'A lot can happen in five months,' she said.

* * *

When Max found Flora later, she was sitting under a vine-covered pergola on a terrace overlooking the sea, busily scribbling in a notebook. Her expression was absorbed, and the afternoon sun filtering through the leaves overhead threw dappled shadows over her face. As he watched, she dropped her pen and notebook into her lap and stretched her arms above her head with a happy sigh as she looked out at the sea.

He must have made an instinctive move towards her because she turned her head, startled, and their eyes met for a long moment before she remembered to lower her arms. 'You're back,' she said.

'Yes.' His own voice sounded hoarse to his ears.

'Good time?' Flora asked as he headed across the terrace to join her.

'Great. The kids were in heaven.' It had been a good day, Max acknowledged, but he had missed her more than he wanted to admit. Holly and Ben had been disappointed that she wasn't there either. He'd had to make up some story about her being tired from the night before. Knowing Holly, she had probably guessed anyway that Flora had a colossal hangover.

'You've caught the sun,' she said.

'You too.' Max grazed her shoulder with his fingertips, where a faint red stripe on the downy skin showed that she had been sitting out too long. The temptation to leave his hand there and slide it down her arm was almost overwhelming, and he made himself snatch it away and sit next to her instead.

He was very aware of the warmth of the sun, the feel of the wooden armrests beneath his hands, the twitter of birds almost drowning out the sound of soldiers marching and presenting arms in the courtyard far below.

'What have you been doing all day?' he asked Flora.

'Recovering from my hangover, mostly,' she admitted. 'But I went down to the kitchen and met the head chef, and asked him how he'd prepared the sea bass last night, so we got talking. He told me about some of San Michele's special dishes, and I've got a few ideas to include in the wedding meal as a nod to Jonas's heritage.' She tapped the notebook on her lap. 'I've got some great ideas for my restaurant too.'

Her restaurant. Right. The one she was going to start as soon as she could. In London. Max kept forgetting that Flora would be moving away. If it wasn't for the ridiculously named cat, she would be gone already, and only zipping back to Combe St Philip to prepare the food for Hope's wedding.

And talking of his sister . . .

'Have you seen Hope today?'

'No. You?'

Max shook his head. 'Carlo came on the boat with us. There was no sign of Hope or Jonas.'

He was worried about his sister, but was reassured when both Jonas and Hope appeared that evening.

★ ★ ★

In contrast to the night before, an informal supper had been planned in the family apartments, or as informally as the Crown Princess could host it. In spite of her chilly adherence to protocol, Anna was clearly a good mother, with three lively children who joined them for supper along with Holly and Ben. The Dowager Princess was allegedly eating in her own apartments. Probably gobbling unwanted visitors, Flora thought, relieved to be spared the risk of another interrogation. Max claimed to have liked the old lady a lot, but then he would.

All the children were overexcited after their day on the boat; which was just as well, Flora reflected, as everyone else was noticeably subdued. She certainly was, perhaps because she stuck to drinking water all evening, but she was worried about Hope too. Max had told her about the way Hope had started to confide in him the night before, but then changed her mind. There was a strained look around Hope's eyes, and she wasn't glowing with happiness the way someone whose engagement to a prince was to be announced in two days' time should be.

When the Crown Princess chivvied the children off to bed, Max went with them to encourage Holly and Ben to behave. The rest of the small party were left with the evening stretching ahead. Nico mentioned a club in the city; the Crown Prince offered a pool table and more drinks in the library; and Hope grew more and more silent. Flora exchanged a glance with Ally, who nodded slightly.

When Crown Prince Carlo asked Flora what she would like to do, she took her opportunity. 'What I'd really like to do is to spend some time alone with Hope and Ally,' she said with her best smile. 'Maybe we could go out together, just the three of us? We haven't had a chance to catch up properly yet.'

The Crown Prince looked uneasy. 'I'm not sure Anna . . . ' he began, but Flora spoke over him, hoping that she wasn't risking the San Michele equivalent of being sent to the Tower.

'Jonas, you can spare her for one evening, can't you?'

'Of course,' he said promptly. 'It's up to Hope, of course. What would you like to do, Hope?'

She hesitated, then she smiled with a trace of her old expression. 'I'd like to go out with Flora and Ally. That's a great idea.'

★   ★   ★

'You may as well put the light on.' Max's voice came out of the darkness as Flora stubbed her toe and failed to stifle a curse.

'I was trying not to wake you,' she said.

'You didn't do a very good job of it,' he grumbled. Reaching out, he switched on the bedside lamp and hauled himself up onto the pillows. He looked rumpled and grumpy and delicious as he squinted at his watch. 'It's nearly two in the morning. What have you been doing?'

'Talking.' Flora sat on the edge of the

271

bed and pulled off her shoes with a wince. They hadn't been any more comfortable two evenings running.

'For *four hours*? What in God's name can you talk about for four hours?'

'Oh, you know . . . ' she said vaguely. 'Girl stuff.'

She didn't tell him how closely Hope and Ally had grilled her about her relationship with Max.

'It was fun,' she told him. 'It's been ages since we've all been out together. We found a fantastic bar.'

'I thought you were never drinking again?'

'I had to. It was my duty as a friend. Hope needed to go out and have a good time. We had cocktails, and there was live music and dancing. It reminded me just how much I like living in a city.'

She padded barefoot into the bathroom to get undressed. She had a pleasant buzz on after a good night out, but there was no denying that she was nervous, too. She wriggled out of her dress and into the camisole and soft shorts that she usually slept in, but when she'd taken off her makeup and done her teeth and used the lavatory, she no reason to lurk any longer. There was nothing to be nervous about anyway, she reminded herself. Max had shown no inclination to jump her, had he?

Unfortunately.

No, wait, that wasn't right. Pull yourself together, Flora, she ordered herself. Hadn't she spent the evening remembering that she was a city girl now? It was the music still throbbing under her skin that was making her heart pound. Nothing to do with the sight of the T-shirt stretched over Max's chest, the faint stubble along his jaw, the powerful arms . . .

Stop it.

Taking a breath, she walked out of the bathroom, and with an assumption of nonchalance, marched over to the bed, her dignity marred only when she tripped over the fringe of one of the Persian carpets, and ended up literally falling onto the mattress.

Max eyed her. 'How many cocktails did you have?'

Four. 'Only a couple,' she said, recovering and scrambling under the covers. There, how hard was that? She was lying right next to Max, not touching him at all. Easy. 'So, how was *your* evening?'

'Very nice, in the end. I went for a walk around the gardens with Celina and her dog.'

'Oh?' Flora bristled. This would be Celina Harris, who was graceful and slender and dark and beautiful and discreet and everything Flora wasn't. 'She has a dog?'

'Yes, a golden retriever called Roscoe. Beautiful dog,' said Max.

Great. Slim, elegant, well-behaved *and* a dog person. Celina was obviously Max's ideal woman.

'Really?'

'She's a very nice woman.' Max shifted on the mattress, making Flora tense. 'Interesting, too.'

'Really?' she said again.

Max didn't seem to notice the chill in her voice. 'Her father was in the US Navy, so she travelled a lot as a child. She's moved around a bit since, too.'

He turned on his side to look at Flora, who was lying with the covers pulled tight under her chin. 'She's a friend of Jonas's. That's how she ended up here.'

'You seem to have had quite a chat.' In the gardens. In the *dark*.

'She got married very young, but she's divorced now.'

'Sounds like you two have a lot in common.'

'Mmm,' said Max, not understanding at all that he was supposed to deny it. 'She's quite private. She was happy to talk about general stuff, but when I asked her about when she got Roscoe, she clammed up. Just said it was a long story.'

'Is she coming to the wedding?'

'I hope so. It'll be nice to have someone sensible to talk to.'

Well, that was *her* put in her place!

Max shifted position so that the mattress dipped, and every cell in Flora's body went on high alert, but all he did was reach across to switch out the light. 'Better get some sleep,' he said as the room was plunged back into darkness.

Sleep, sure. How could she sleep when Max was *right there*? Flora could feel his warmth, only inches away, could hear him breathing, slow and steady. He clearly wasn't bothered by the fact that she was lying there, vibrating like a tuning fork, while he dropped easily back to sleep.

He was so close. It would be so easy to reach out and lay her palm on his firmly turned back. The temptation to wriggle over and press herself into his back was overwhelming. She could slip her hands beneath his T-shirt and kiss the back of his neck, drifting round to his jaw until he rolled over . . .

Or she could not. A sigh leaked out of Flora. Very, very cautiously, she wriggled to the edge of the bed and turned her back to Max, putting herself firmly out of temptation's way.

★ ★ ★

Flora surfaced, feeling warm and safe and deliciously comfortable. There was a warm weight over her, pinning her into softness. A hard, solid body was pressed into her back, a warm hand holding her firmly in place. Puffs of breath tickled her bare shoulder, and a pair of hairily muscled masculine legs were tangled in hers.

She blinked at the faint light striping through the curtains. There was an annoying buzzing coming from some-where. A phone. Flora didn't want to move. She lay still, pretending that she couldn't hear it.

Behind her, Max mumbled in his sleep and pulled her closer, and oh, it felt good. She should probably wake him and remind him who she was, Flora thought, but surely a few more minutes like this couldn't do any harm? What would he do if she rolled over, and pressed even closer? Her body was clamouring: do it, do it, do it. Her blood was pounding, her skin pulsing, every inch of her itching and yearning. What if she did? Would he smile and pull her into him and kiss her?

The phone kept buzzing. To hell with it, Flora decided. She started to turn just as Max stirred. Too late. She felt him wake, felt him realize just where his hands were, felt him register that his phone was ringing.

With a muttered curse, he rolled away from her and flailed on the bedside table for the phone. 'What?' he snarled into it, while Flora hastily adjusted her plan and put on what she thought was a rather good imitation of someone coming round from a deep sleep instead, stirring lazily, yawning, a languid hand rubbing her eyes.

'What?' Max said again in a different voice. 'You're *what?*'

Flora abandoned her improvisation

and struggled up into a sitting position. This didn't sound good. Max was sitting on the side of the bed, the phone clamped to his ear, his other hand dragging though his hair.

'But why? I thought . . . No, don't do that,' said hastily. 'Just go. Don't worry about anything. We'll sort it out this end.' He paused, listening. 'I just want you to be happy. That's all that matters.'

Switching off the phone, he dropped it back onto the table and looked over his shoulder at Flora. It was clear that kissing her was the last thing on his mind. 'What in God's name did you two say to Hope last night?'

'What do you mean?'

'She and Jonas have run away.'

'*What?*' Flora's jaw dropped. '*Why?*'

'She just said she and Jonas needed to talk. Are you sure she didn't say anything last night?'

'No. Ally and I both asked her if she was okay or wanted to talk, and she said she didn't. She said she just wanted to be ordinary again, so we were.'

Max rubbed a hand over his face. 'The formal announcement of the engagement is at the ball tomorrow. Celina was telling me about all the arrangements. It's not going to be much of a ball without the engaged couple, is it?'

At least Hope's news had driven the awkwardness of waking up entwined out of their heads. Flora sent Ally a text and she came to the room before breakfast, looking as worried as they were.

'What are we going to do?'

'We'll have to carry on as normal,' said Max. 'I don't think anyone else knows about this. We could take the kids somewhere. What about you?'

'I've got some interviews,' said Ally. 'You can say you think they're with me, and I'll say I think they're with you. Maybe no one will notice?' she said hopefully.

But the Crown Princess was already fretting at Jonas and Hope's absence. 'I can't think what's happened to them!'

The Dowager Princess had been watching the exchange of glances between Flora and Ally. 'Don't fuss, Anna,' she said unexpectedly. 'I've told them to take Max and Flora to the summer palace and give them lunch there.'

'Oh, Grandmamma! There's so much to do before the ball!'

'Nonsense, everything's perfectly organized.'

When Max, Flora and the Dowager were left alone at last, she regarded them severely. 'So Hope's bolted, has she? I wondered if she would.'

'She hasn't *bolted*,' said Max. 'She and Jonas are just . . . having some time alone.'

The Dowager's sniff showed what she thought of that. 'Well, it's up to my grandson. I wouldn't underestimate him. There's no point in telling Anna that, though. She'd just flap. You'd better go and pretend Jonas and Hope are with you. I'll send Celina to make the arrangements.'

So Flora and Max found themselves in a helicopter with Celina and with Holly and Ben, who at least were thrilled by the treat. They flew through pristine valleys and over spectacular mountains and landed at last at a beautiful palace mirrored in a lake, vineyards crowding behind it. If Flora hadn't been so worried, she would have loved it, but as it was, she kept checking her phone in case Hope had been in touch.

She couldn't help wishing that Celina wasn't there as well; not because she wasn't nice — she was. Too nice. Graceful, stylish, friendly without being pushy, competent without being bossy. She had a quiet sense of humour, but Flora thought there was a sadness there too, and wondered about her marriage. What sort of man had been able to bowl cool, calm Celina off her feet?

But if Celina hadn't been there, they could have been a family.

Back in Liburno, they ate at a waterside restaurant and slunk back to the palace, hoping not to meet anyone who would expect to see Jonas and Hope with them.

'It's exhausting being conspirators.' Flora flopped onto the bed when they got back to the room at last. They had left Holly and Ben in the children's apartments with a capable nanny who promised to ensure that they were scrubbed clean and dressed in their best clothes to put in an appearance at the opening of the ball.

Max sat on the edge of the bed and pulled off his shoes. 'The whole situation is ridiculous,' he said irritably. 'What are we doing in a palace in San Michele, running around trying to hoodwink Crown Princesses? It's mad.'

Flora's phone beeped to signal a text and she scrabbled for it. 'Is that Hope?' Max asked.

'I hope so . . . oh . . . no, it's Ally's mum. She's sent a photo of Sweetie to reassure me that he's okay.' She showed Max the picture of Sweetie squinting malevolently at the camera.

'Thank God for that!' Max didn't even bother to hide his sarcasm and Flora stuck her tongue out at him.

'Who's looking after Bella and Ted?'

'They're staying with Stella. She's got dogs of her own, so they'll be okay.'

'I bet you've had updates on how *they* are.'

'Daily,' he admitted, swinging his legs up onto the bed and settling himself more comfortably against the pillows, 'but they're dogs, so it's different.'

'*Right.*'

He grinned at her expression, and after a moment she smiled back, which felt oddly companionable until at the same instant they both seemed to realize that they were alone on a bed and smiling at each other, and their smiles faded and suddenly there didn't seem to be enough oxygen in the room.

Kiss me. The words rang so loudly in her head that for one terrible moment Flora thought that she must have spoken aloud, but as the silence lengthened, it was Max who looked away first. 'I'll text Hope again,' he said abruptly, and swung his legs off the bed once more.

'I'll go and get ready,' said Flora, equally cool (she hoped). 'We haven't got that long before the ball.'

In the bathroom, she stared into the mirror. She shouldn't be obsessing about touching Max when Hope was missing. It wasn't as if anything had changed. It felt different because they were away from Combe St Philip, but he was getting texts from Stella every day. Did that sound like a man ready to move on? And while her grandparents' beloved cat was still alive, she needed the manor kitchen. Much better to be sensible and keep things professional.

14

By the time Max had showered, shaved and dressed in the bathroom, Flora was at the mirror, head tilted to one side as she fixed in her earrings, and the sight of her made his heart stumble alarmingly. She wore a dark blue ball gown that left her creamy shoulders bare, and gave her an elegance he had never seen before.

Sensing his gaze, she turned. 'Look, no bright colours.' She shook out the long skirts with a tentative smile. 'What do you think?'

Max thought that if he wasn't supposed to be turning up and explaining to a fretful Crown Princess why his sister had gone missing from her own engagement party, he would have dragged Flora over to the bed there and then and showed her what he thought.

'I think you look beautiful,' he said simply, and the colour rushed up into her face.

'Thank you,' she said awkwardly.

His sincerity had obviously thrown her. It probably would have been easier to stick to their usual banter, but Max was tired, tired of reminding himself of all the reasons why he shouldn't touch Flora the way he so badly wanted to.

Flora forced a smile. 'Since we're being polite, you look pretty good yourself.'

Max looked down at himself in surprise. He had on a white shirt, still open at the throat, dark trousers and a cummerbund, and the black tie was draped around his neck ready to be tied.

'It's so unfair,' she went on. 'Women have to go to a huge amount of effort to look good, but men just have to put on a dinner jacket to look a million times better.'

'It's not all easy,' said Max. 'Ties are just another form of torture, and I've been struggling with these cufflinks.' He lifted his wrists to show his cuffs. 'Hope gave them to me, so I thought I should wear them, but I'd forgotten what a pain they are to fasten.'

'Here, let me have a go.' Flora walked over to him, very conscious of the silky fabric swishing around her legs like a caress. It was the most expensive dress she had ever bought, but when she had seen Max's face, it had been worth it.

I think you look beautiful.

As briskly as possible, she took hold of his wrist and tried to slip the cufflink into the buttonholes. His nearness was distracting. She could smell him, clean cotton and clean male skin, and feel the strength of his arm. In her heels, her face was on a level with his, and although she tried to keep her eyes fixed on the cuff, the edge of his jaw snagged at the corner of her gaze, and no matter how hard she focused on the wretched cufflink, all she could think about was how easy it would be to look up and lean just a little closer, to turn her head, just a little, to press her mouth to his.

Flora swallowed hard. One cufflink done, thank God. She turned her attention to the other wrist when Max obligingly held his arm up. His chest was rising and falling steadily, and she wondered if he could hear her galloping heart or the thrum of hazy excitement beneath her skin. Desire clenched like a fist in her belly.

At last. The second cufflink was fastened into place.

'Thanks,' said Max in a strained voice.

Flora's pulse was a deafening boom, but from somewhere she dredged up the strength to step back. They had a ball to go to, and if Hope didn't reappear, things were going to get very difficult.

She summoned a smile. 'We'd better go. Holly and Ben will be waiting.'

Max's hands were not quite steady as he fixed his tie and shrugged into his dinner jacket. He was tempted to damn the ball, but Flora was right. His children were waiting, and his sister was God knew where. There was a potential disaster to be averted. He couldn't stay here and peel that dress off Flora.

Because it was such a special occasion, all the children except for little Katja had been invited to the opening of the ball. Not that Ben appreciated the honour. Resentful at being scrubbed up, he stood in the corner with the young princes while Holly twirled and showed off the dress that Stella had bought her specially. It brought her lots of compliments that she accepted with a quite alarming composure.

'Where's Hope?' Holly's clear voice rang through the crowd. 'I want her to see my dress!'

It was a good question, and unfortunately Crown Princess Anna had heard it. 'Yes, where *is* Hope?' she asked, frowning. 'Everybody's here except her and Jonas. It's too bad of them to be late.'

'Well . . . ' Max cleared his throat,

and was preparing to make a clean breast of it when Flora touched his arm. When he glanced at her, she was smiling, and he followed her gaze to the door where Hope stood with Jonas.

One by one, everyone in the room stopped talking and turned and a hush fell over the room. Jonas's face blazed with triumph, but it was Hope's expression that made Max's throat close. She was stunning, glowing with happiness as she held Jonas's arm. Her copper hair tumbled free to her shoulders, and she looked every inch a princess. Relief, love and pride in her clamped like a tight band around Max's chest.

Without realizing what he was doing, Max took Flora's hand and squeezed it. 'It's going to be okay,' he said, and she nodded as she squeezed back.

★ ★ ★

It was a magical evening. A spectacular buffet that had Flora clucking with approval was laid out in one of the

291

reception rooms, while the dancing took place in a staggeringly ornate ballroom. Under the chandeliers, the women's dresses were a kaleidoscope of colour. Their hair was decorated with glittering tiaras, and jewels glowed at their ears and throats. The San Michele princes and other nobles wore lavish uniforms that were almost as beautiful as some of the dresses, but many of the men like Max wore dinner jackets, the plain black and white a perfect foil for all the extravagance, colour and glitz.

Holly was persuaded reluctantly to bed at last, after making Flora promise faithfully to tell her everything about the ball the next day. Ben and the two princes had made an earlier escape, leaving Max and Flora at last with no responsibilities, both giddy with relief at not having to worry about Hope any longer.

They stood together to watch Jonas and Hope dance the traditional slow waltz alone, and then, when the band struck up a livelier tune and everyone took to the floor, it seemed completely natural when Max turned to her. 'Let's dance,' he said.

All evening, Flora had been agonizingly aware of him. Max, with his lean, tough body. Max with his stern face and imperious nose. She couldn't drag her gaze from the hard, exciting line of his cheek, the heart-shaking angle of his jaw, the cool, firm line of his mouth set in a way that sent heat rolling through her. And now here he was, holding out his hand, and when she took it, he eased a way for them through the guests now crowding onto the dance floor around Jonas and Hope.

'I thought you couldn't dance?' she said, raising her voice over the music and the laughter and chatter.

'I can't,' he said. 'But I can hold you.'

There was a short, sizzling silence between them, then Flora moved in to him and put one hand on his shoulder. 'So you can,' she said.

'Wooden' would normally be a good way to describe Max on the dance floor, but with Flora in his arms it didn't matter. She fit perfectly against him as if she had been made for him. He rested his cheek against her temple and smelled the light summery scent of her hair and he thought about the way she smiled, the way his heart eased when she was in the room. He thought about the way she had kissed him, and desire thudded in his heart. He wanted to tangle his fingers in her hair and drag her mouth to his, to lose himself in her softness and her warmth.

Enough with the dancing. He wanted her to himself. 'Let's go,' he said before the first number had ended.

Flora pulled back slightly. Her eyes were dark, and he knew that she had been thinking the same as he had. 'Do you think we can?'

Max took her hand in a firm grip. 'My sister's going to be a princess,' he said. 'We can do whatever we like.'

They slipped out of the ballroom, leaving the dancers to their music, and hurried down the sweeping marble staircase. Never had the way back to their room seemed so long. By the time they got to their corridor, they were walking faster and faster until they were almost running. Max fumbled with the handle and pulled Flora through, swinging her round so that he could close the door and press her back against it to kiss her with desperate, hungry kisses.

'You know how we decided that this would be a bad idea?'

'Mmn?' Flora blizzarded kisses along his jaw as she groped at the buttons on his shirt, desperate to get at his skin beneath, reduced to tugging the shirt-tails out of his trousers instead.

Max cupped her face between his hands and made her pause and look at him.

'I've changed my mind,' he said raggedly.

Flora's answering smile made his heart swell. 'So have I,' she said.

★   ★   ★

When Flora woke the next morning, bright sunlight was angling through a chink in the shutters and slanting across the floor. 'Remind me again why we thought this would be a bad idea?' Max murmured. He was kissing his way along Flora's shoulder to press his mouth to the sweet angle of her neck, making her arch and shudder with pleasure. There were worse ways to be woken up.

'Um . . . ' Flora was replete and satisfied, as languidly relaxed as a cat stretching in the sunshine. 'Weren't we afraid it would make things awkward?' she suggested lazily.

'I don't feel awkward, do you?'

With an effort, she engaged her brain and rolled onto her side to face him. 'We might when we get back to Combe St Philip,' she made herself say.

'Perhaps.' Max skimmed his hand over her hip. 'But we're not home yet. This place doesn't seem real somehow. The normal rules don't apply.'

'What goes on in the palace, stays in

the palace?' Flora suggested, and a smile touched his mouth.

'Exactly. Once we're back to reality, we can pretend this never happened. We'll draw a line when go home,' said Max. 'We can be sensible then.'

Flora couldn't imagine ever forgetting the night they had just spent, but Max was right. Things would probably seem different when they were back in Combe St Philip.

'Okay,' she said. 'It's just one more thing to pretend, and we've got so good at pretending it's hard to remember what's real and what isn't now.'

'I know what you mean,' said Max with feeling. 'Are we or are we not engaged, for instance? I keep losing track.'

'We are for the next twenty-four hours,' said Flora. 'We're madly in love until our flight home, and then we stop.'

His warm hand moved possessively over her. 'The flight back isn't until tomorrow,' he pointed out, and she smiled and moved closer to wind her arms around his neck.

'We might as well make the most of being engaged then, don't you think?' she said, and Max smiled too as he rolled her beneath him.

'I think we should,' he agreed.

⋆　⋆　⋆

Afterwards, Flora was hard put to say exactly what they had done that last day in San Michele. It passed in a blur of laughter and a shimmering, bone-melting awareness of Max beside her, and all she remembered was the leap of her senses whenever he so much as grazed her hand with his own. The deep throb of anticipation. The longing to say goodnight to everyone and go back to their room. Max's smile when he closed the door behind him. 'Come here,' he said, and she went.

But all too soon the night was over, and they were packing in silence. Reality seeped in with the daylight, and with it the knowledge that this magical interlude was over.

When her phone beeped, Flora actually jumped. 'It's Ally,' she said puzzled. 'I wondered where she'd got to . . . '

'Don't tell me *she's* disappeared now!' said Max.

'She wants me to pack her pack for her.' Flora was reading the text. 'She'll see us at the airport.'

She texted back: *Where r u?*

But there was no reply.

At least packing for Ally took her mind off the fact that she was never going to touch Max again. They had agreed. What went on in San Michele, stayed in San Michele. It had been fun, but it was better to draw a line now rather than prolong the inevitable ending in the cold light of reality. Their lives were too different. They wanted different things. It would never work. Oh, there were so many reasons to be sensible! It was pointless to wish that they could stay in San Michele forever.

Ally nearly missed the flight. She ran across the tarmac just as the steps to the plane were about to be towed away.

Out of breath, she sent Flora a quick grateful smile. *Tell you later*, she mouthed as she hurried down the gangway and flung herself into the seat at the back, where she fell asleep almost before the plane had taken off. In truth, Flora wasn't sorry to postpone a conversation with her friend. Ally would know at once that something momentous had happened, and Flora didn't want to talk about those two magical nights with Max. She had to pretend they had never happened.

If she could.

It was raining when they landed at Bristol, a dreary depressing drizzle that seemed to punish them for the sunshine in San Michele. There were no luxurious limousines to meet them now, only the hassle of finding the car in the car park, sitting in traffic jams and dealing with fractious and overtired children.

'It doesn't take long to get back to reality, does it?' said Max, grim-faced at the steering wheel as they edged through roadworks.

Flora looked out of the window as the windscreen wipers slapped back and forth. 'No,' she said. 'No, it doesn't.'

* * *

Sweetie mewed so piteously when Flora let herself into the cottage that she bent cautiously and picked him up, half-expecting to be savaged for her presumption. Instead of scratching and wriggling free as he usually did, he purred, and she buried her face in his soft fur. 'Did you miss me, puss?' Was it her imagination, or was he thinner?

Max hadn't even switched off the engine when he'd dropped her off. He carried her case to the door, but all he said was, 'See you tomorrow.' Holly and Ben had been sitting in the back of the car, so they hadn't been able to talk;

and anyway, what was there to say? They had both agreed to draw a line when they got home.

He'd left her at the cottage to drive straight to Stella's, to drop off the children and pick up the dogs.

To pick up his life that didn't include her.

But she had a life of her own too, Flora reminded herself as she fed Sweetie and loaded the washing machine. She had good friends and a great career, and a chance one day soon to open an incredible restaurant, the restaurant she had been dreaming about since she was seven.

And before that, the prestige of catering a royal wedding, no less. She had picked up some great ideas from the palace chef. There had been no opportunity to talk about menus in San Michele, but now Hope and Jonas were officially engaged, the wedding preparations could begin in earnest. Hope would be coming over in a few weeks, and they could make some decisions.

She would need to hire some more fridges and hobs for the wedding itself, Flora reckoned, and some assistants too. She must start thinking about that soon.

So she really didn't have time to mope about Max. They had drawn a line, and she would stick to it.

Flora had a bright smile ready when he came into the kitchen next day. True, the sight of him brought a flash of feeling so intense that for a moment she couldn't speak, but the next moment she had recovered and was able to offer him a coffee in a voice that sounded almost unnaturally steady.

It was almost as if they had never been away. Max was taciturn, taking his coffee away with him to his study. Nobody would ever have guessed that he had rolled her beneath him and teased kisses across her belly, that he had smiled as his hands moved hungrily over her, sending pleasure spooling through her. Flora told herself that tiny shiver under her skin was because it was cold, and nothing to do with the memory of how good he had felt, of the hard press of his body, the devastating warmth of his mouth.

She refused to let herself remember. There was no point in remembering. As time passed, Flora reminded herself of that every day. She cooked and she baked and she made notes; but still, every time she heard the back door or the skitter of dog claws on the quarry tiles, her heart lurched into her throat and the memories came crowding back anyway.

It might be awkward, she had said, and it was. Day by day, the tension grew until it was suffocating, blotting out all attempts to behave naturally. Max's visits to the kitchen grew briefer and briefer.

Just as well, Flora told herself, but she missed him. She missed the sardonic tone, the roll of his eyes, his long fingers curled around the mug. She missed the way he had smiled at her in San Michele.

For the first time in her life, Flora lost her appetite. She was bored with baking, and lost all her inspiration for the wedding menu. It was just food, after all. Who cared about flavour? People just wanted to eat. They didn't care about colour or texture or seasoning.

Almost a week dragged past. It was raining again, a slow, steady drip onto the tiles outside, and Flora was beating eggs drearily when the back door banged, followed by hasty steps along the passage. The kitchen door opened. Max stood there, framed in the doorway, looking grim.

Flora stopped beating. 'What on earth's the matter?'

'You,' he said, striding towards her. 'Or maybe it's me.' He took the bowl from her and plonked it on the table. 'I've changed my mind. I don't want to be sensible,' he said as her mouth dropped open. 'I've spent my whole life being sensible. Now I want to make a fool of myself over you.'

Hauling Flora towards him, he kissed her furiously, as if she had driven him to distraction, and after an astounded moment, Flora wound her arms around him and kissed him back, as hungry as he was. The fetters clamping her to reality had snapped open, freeing her in a glorious, giddy rush. Half-laughing, half-desperate, they grabbed at each other, ripping and tugging at clothes, kissing frantically, stumbling back to the kitchen table, where they both lost control completely in the nicest possible way.

★   ★   ★

'Dear God,' said Max afterwards, his face buried in her neck, his voice ragged. 'What have you done to me?'

'Me?' Flora pretended outrage as they disentangled themselves. 'I was just beating eggs when you came in and whirled me over to the kitchen table! That was *so* unhygienic,' she added. 'Don't do it again. Or not very often.'

'Sorry.' Max helped her straighten her clothes. 'I wasn't thinking. That's the trouble. I can't think when you're around, and I can't think when you're not.'

Deeply pleased, Flora adjusted his collar. 'I know what you mean.'

'Look, I know nothing's changed,' he said. 'I know you're not planning to be around forever, but while you *are* around . . . why don't we make the most of it?'

It was perfect, Flora told herself. She and Max agreed a no-strings affair to get each other out of their systems. There would be no commitment, and they would keep their independence.

Although Max was cross when she got out of bed later that night and got dressed.

'Where are you going?'

'Home.'

'Why don't you stay?'

'I need to be with Sweetie,' she said. 'He's a bit off his food.'

'He's just manipulating you. Cats are

sneaky that way.'

Flora bent down to kiss him. 'I promised Pops I'd look after him. I don't think he likes being left on his own. He's taken to sleeping with me, and he'll miss me if I'm not there.'

'He's not the only one,' Max grumbled, getting up and pulling on his trousers.

'What are you doing?' asked Flora, puzzled.

'Walking you home. It's late.'

* * *

For the next few weeks, Max complained about playing second fiddle to a cat, but he didn't try to persuade Flora to stay the night again. That was clearly going to be a losing battle. The dogs joyfully adapted to a late-night walk, and escorting Flora to her cottage every night was a small price to pay for being able to hold her again.

It wasn't just in his bedroom that life had changed. Workmen had started on the renovations and redecoration in preparation for Hope's wedding. Ally kept the office he had given her to organize PR around the wedding, and was often to be seen running up and down the stairs, clipboard in hand, a phone clamped to her ear, usually too busy to do more than wave at Max as she passed. But even she wasn't the real reason Hasebury Hall felt as if it was getting a new lease of life. It was because of Flora, with her laughter and her huge capacity for love.

He just wasn't sure whether she loved him.

And why should she? ran the doubting voice in Max's head. His mother hadn't, and in the end, Stella hadn't either. Why should Flora be any different? She wasn't a dog, offering unconditional love for no reason at all; and what, really, did he have to offer her?

Flora was too bright a star to stay in Combe St Philip, anyway. The cakes and tarts she produced were exquisite, and she talked still about her dream of owning a restaurant one day. Having held on to his own dream of the manor, Max understood what that meant to her. It wouldn't be fair to stand in her way and make it difficult for her to leave.

But for now, there were still three months until the wedding. Three months until she would think about leaving. Max intended to make the most of them.

*   *   *

Spring was definitely in the air. The incessant rain earlier in the year had given way to a mild, pale sunshine, and the daffodils were bursting out in the new warmth. Bella and Ted at his heels, Max made his way back from the greenhouses. He had been up early to check the plants there and needed to get on with a design for landscaping a new hospital, but he might as well get a coffee first. It was pathetic, the way he found excuses to pop in and see Flora.

As soon as he opened the back door, though, he knew that she wasn't there. The kitchen was cold and empty. He checked his phone, but there was no message. Concerned, he whistled for Ted and Bella, and walked down to the village.

'It's open,' said Flora dully at the sound of his knock.

The door opened into the little sitting room. Flora was sitting in a chair, Sweetie on her lap, and when she looked at Max, her face was blank and white.

'He's dead,' she said in a voice he barely recognized. 'I thought that I was waiting for him to die, but now that he has, I can't bear it. I can't bear it.'

The cat's body was already stiffening. Max found a towel, wrapped Sweetie gently in it and lifted him from Flora's lap. Then he picked up Flora and carried her to the other chair so that he could hold her while she cried.

His sunny Flora. Max's heart cracked

to hear her weep. 'I'm sorry, I'm sorry,' she kept saying. 'I shouldn't be crying.'

'Flora, it's nothing to be ashamed of. I know you loved Sweetie.'

'But I didn't really love him,' she wailed. 'I don't understand why I'm even crying, when I didn't cry like this for Granny or for Pops.'

Max suspected that she hadn't let herself cry. She would have been too busy putting on a smile and appearing cheerful for everyone at the funeral.

'You're grieving for them now. Sweetie was your last link to them. You're allowed to be sad.'

'I've been so lucky,' she sobbed. She swiped at her cheeks with the back of her hand. 'I could have been dragged around from commune to cult for years if Granny and Pops hadn't taken me in. I'm just so grateful to them, and they hated seeing me cry,' she said tearfully. 'They'd *hate* seeing me now . . . '

Max's throat tightened. He thought about the brave little girl, abandoned by her careless mother, rewarding her grandparents with a cheerful smile that hid the sadness she must surely have felt.

'Flora, they would understand,' he said. 'They loved Sweetie too, didn't they? And you looked after him, right to the end, just like you promised you would.'

'What am I going to do with him now?' Flora's tears had quietened to hiccupping sobs. 'I don't know where to bury him. The garden's so small here. I don't want anyone to dig him up by mistake.'

'I tell you what,' said Max. 'We'll bury him in the orchard at the manor, and we'll get him a headstone, like all the other animals there.'

'But you told me that there are only dogs buried there.'

'We'll make Sweetie an honorary dog.' Max could see his own dogs sitting quietly, sensing the atmosphere. 'He saw off Bella and Ted, didn't he?'

That won him a watery smile at last. So they carried Sweetie up to the

313

orchard, and Max took a spade and dug a hole next to the grave of his beloved Bess, while Flora crouched down and read the names lovingly carved on the stones: Rex, Major, Ajax, Roger, Mungo, Meg . . . 'Oh, dear, 'Sweetie' rather lowers the tone,' she said.

Max was glad to hear her sounding more her old self. He had hated seeing her cry, *hated* it. But it wasn't fair that she felt she always had to be cheerful, and he had felt the strangest urge to gather her up and make everything right for her.

He couldn't bring Sweetie back to life, but he could at least give the old cat a decent resting place. He didn't think the dogs would mind. Sweetie's place in the orchard would be a permanent link to Flora, too. Even if she went away, as she had always said she would, he would be able to think of her here, trying to smile through her devastation, grieving for a cat that had scratched her and bitten her and trapped her, but that she had loved anyway.

Flora had such a huge capacity for loving, Max had come to realize. It was selfish — and pointless — to want to keep that love just for himself. One day she would go and build the career she so deserved, and it would be wrong of him to deny her that. But while she was here, he could at least support her, the way she supported everyone else.

Max put his foot on the spade and lifted out another clod of earth. He might not be very good with words or emotions, but he could be practical; and if that meant digging a grave for Sweetie, then that was what he would do.

15

Max probably regretted telling her that she was allowed to be sad sometimes. It felt to Flora as if she wept for days afterwards. She hadn't realized how much sadness she had bottled up inside her. She had been too busy helping her grandfather after her grandmother died to grieve properly herself, and when he had died in his turn, she had been projecting all the attention she had given him onto the cat. It had been easier to think about practical things — dealing with probate, thinking about what to do about the cottage or how to keep her catering business afloat — than to remember that the kindly, steady grandfather with the twinkle in his eye was no more.

Max was more patient than she could have possibly imagined. He mopped her up, made her cups of tea, made her laugh, and then held her at night when she cried again. No longer did she have to climb out of a warm bed to walk home to the cottage; now she could spend all night with Max, and it began to feel perilously like the relationship that neither of them claimed to want.

'You're free now,' Max tried to comfort her when she began to wobble again one night. 'You can sell the cottage, do whatever you want.'

'I can't do anything until after the wedding,' Flora objected.

'The wedding's only three months away,' he pointed out. 'If you're serious about starting that restaurant, there's lots you could be doing in the meantime. I imagine it'll take a lot longer than three months to find premises and sort out the money side of things, let alone promote a new place and plan the food and decor.'

He was right. Flora had been using Sweetie, along with Hope's wedding, to mark time. She could see that now. It had been good to have a few months to regroup, but it was time now to get moving again. It would be too easy to stay comfortably here in Combe St Philip and forget the dreams that had kept her going for so long, especially when she was waking up next to Max every morning.

But it felt as if Max was encouraging her to go back to London. He had been clear from the start that whatever they had would only be temporary, Flora remembered, mortified. They had had a good time, and he had been more than kind, but perhaps it was time for her to think about going.

Max himself was busy with design work, and overseeing the production of plants in the greenhouses. She suspected that he was working harder to pay for the renovations to the manor. The house was swarming with plumbers, electricians and decorators who were smartening rooms in preparation for the wedding. Even the great hall was getting a fresh coat of paint above the panelling. The moth-eaten stag heads had been taken down, Flora was relieved to see, and the empty hall itself was now stunning in its space and simplicity, making a virtue out of necessity.

Flora loved seeing the old house come to life after being neglected for so long. She was kept busy providing mugs of tea and biscuits, and happily offered advice and sometimes decisions. Max's idea of décor was to paint everything white; and while that could look stunning, as in the great hall, Flora couldn't help feeling that the other rooms called for some warmer colour. She loved walking along the crooked corridors with their up-and-down steps and unexpected turns. The bedrooms were as quirky as the rest of the house, some with beamed ceilings and sloping floors, others built in the 'new' eighteenth-century extension with gracious windows overlooking the gardens.

But these weren't rooms she was ever going to live in, Flora had to keep reminding herself. She paused on a landing, her hands full of empty mugs she had collected earlier, and looked through the mullioned window to the walled garden below. It was April already, and the plants were budding up nicely in the spring sunshine. In a few weeks, the garden would be a haze of green — and a few weeks after *that*, the borders would be in full bloom. The roses would be out and a grand marquee would be erected on the lawn, and it would be full of laughing, chattering guests drinking champagne and tucking into the canapes Flora had planned. Hope would be married to her prince.

And Flora would have no reason to stay any longer.

Her future was in London, not in a sleepy village. Flora opened her laptop that evening and contacted friends in the restaurant business. She was coming back soon, she said, and was ready for a fresh start. Who could she sound out about investment?

The reply, when it came, threw her completely.

'*Rich?*' Max echoed in disbelief when she told him. 'As in the boyfriend who dumped you for caring about your grandfather? *That* Rich?'

'I know, I was surprised too.'

'Why are you even writing to him?'

'I didn't. A friend must have told him that I'd been in touch. But he says that he's in talks with investors about a place in Notting Hill Gate. We used to talk about having a restaurant together, and he wants me to think about going in with him. It would be a purely business relationship, obviously.'

'Oh, obviously,' Max sneered. 'I can't believe you'd even consider it after the way he treated you.'

'He's a brilliant chef,' said Flora simply.

'There's more to life than cooking.'

'Not if you're planning a top restaurant. Look, you were the one who said I should get moving,' she pointed out crossly. 'And you were right. I've drifted for long enough. I need to be thinking about going back to London. Obviously the wedding is my priority, but I've put the cottage on the market, and it's time to start thinking about what I'm going to do. I'm not going to be stuck in Combe St Philip for the rest of my life. All I've ever wanted is to run a brilliant restaurant, and now I've got an opportunity to do just that. Rich might not be the most reliable person when it comes to relationships, but he's a rising star in the restaurant world. I'd never get close to the kind of investment he has access to.

'I couldn't believe it when he first suggested we went into business together last year. Then it was like a dream come true, like Hope finding a real-life prince and becoming a princess. Of course it won't be the same now that we've split up, but still, the fact that he'd still consider me as a partner in the kitchen . . . it's an amazing opportunity.'

Max was unconvinced, but what had he expected? *Amazing*, Flora had said, stars in her eyes. Rich was her prince, the brilliant cook with all the contacts and the pizzazz to launch the restaurant she wanted. She'd go back to her London life, just the way she had always said that she wanted to. He'd tried to be unselfish and comfort her, but he'd been fooling himself. All along he had been hoping that she would want to stay . . . but why would she stay for *him*?

For a horrible moment, Max felt like a little boy again, deposited by his parents at school like an unwanted parcel. Which was absurd. He was a grown man, and he certainly didn't need Flora.

Flora was burbling on about her restaurant, about the dishes she would cook and the sensation they would cause. 'I said I'd go up and meet him next week to talk about it,' she said. 'I'm in a bit of a lull as far as the catering goes, and I can freeze a lot in advance.'

'What about the wedding?'

'Don't worry about that. I've been in touch with Hope, and I'm going to cook a taster session for her when she comes over in a couple of weeks, but she says she trusts me to decide on the menu.'

'If that's the case, why don't you take a few days?' said Max. 'Setting up a restaurant isn't something you can do over lunch.'

'Yes, I suppose I could do that,' said Flora. 'I've got friends I could stay with.'

Of course she did. She was a city girl.

I'm not going to be stuck in Combe St Philip for the rest of my life, she had said.

There was an awkward pause, and then they both spoke at the same time.

'Look — '

'Max — '

'You first,' he said.

'No, you go.'

He hesitated. 'I'm thinking that this may be the time when we should call it a day,' he said, while in the back of his mind a voice was shouting: *No! No! What are you saying? Shut up now!*

'That's what I was going to say.'

Flora seemed relieved. 'It's better to end it now while we can still be friends, isn't it?'

'Exactly. Not that it hasn't been . . . ' Incredible, heart-shaking, amazing. ' . . . fun, but we always knew it was really just a holiday fling.'

'You've been so lovely about Sweetie,' said Flora, 'but it's not as if we've got anything in common,' she reminded him with a wavering smile.

Except the way they moved together, in each other, around each other. Except that when they held each other, the world went away.

'We can keep our fake engagement going for the wedding,' she went on. 'We don't want Anna getting in a tizzy about her seating plans, but that's not going to be a problem if we're still friends and can end things in a civilized way.'

Civilized. Max stared at the door after she left, a red mist behind his eyes. He didn't feel civilized, he felt like tearing down the door with his bare hands and storming after her, spinning her round and shouting at her that he wouldn't let her go, that she had to stay right there with him. How dare she smile and say they would be friends? How dare she leave him alone?

His jaw was locked with the effort of not yelling, and he wanted to punch something, but when he looked down, his vision cleared enough to see Bella and Ted watching him, doggy eyebrows twitching in concern. They helped him take a breath, then another.

No, it was all for the best. This was his home, where he belonged. He had fought long and hard to keep Hasebury Hall safe. Stella would say that he had sacrificed his marriage for it. Holly and Ben were here. Bella and Ted were here. His work was here.

He had been perfectly happy here without Flora, and he would be again.

'We'll be fine,' he told the dogs.

They didn't look convinced.

★   ★   ★

'What do you think?' Rich looked at her eagerly.

Flora looked around the space. It managed to be large and yet intimate at the same time, with different levels and big industrial windows letting in lots of light. It felt airy and welcoming and she could picture it so clearly filled with tables and diners, the air humming with the excitement of great food served in funky yet comfortable surroundings.

She managed a smile. 'It's perfect,' she said.

And it was. It was everything she'd ever dreamed of. So why wasn't she more excited about it?

The Notting Hill Gate property hadn't been suitable in the end, and Rich had persuaded her to consider this converted warehouse in Docklands, overlooking the Thames. 'This is groovier,' he had insisted, and Flora could see that he was right. It wasn't an area she knew well, but it had an edgy appeal, and she liked being able to see the river.

She had been back in London a

week, staying with friends and rediscovering the city. There was still so much about it that she loved: the way majestic old buildings jostled with the new, the purposeful way Londoners walked, the hubbub of languages around her. She loved the parks and the red buses, the elegant Georgian squares and the pretty painted houses. There was a vibrancy to the city streets that she had missed in Combe St Philip, that sense of a place where anything might happen.

But the more she tried to tell herself how much she liked the Thames, the more she remembered the little river that ran through the water-meadows. She would stand on one of the great London bridges and remember the bridge in Combe St Philip. In the summer you could lean over the parapet to catch the flash of a fish darting through the clear water, and listen to the sheep bleating on the downs. Walking through Hyde Park, all she could think about was walking along the ridgeway with the valley sweeping away.

It was good to be back in London, but she missed the greenness of the village. She was horribly homesick for the froth of cow parsley along the hedgerows and the smell of the long grass after the rain. For the burble of the river and the peal of bells on a Sunday morning. The clip-clop of horses' hooves and the way old Mrs Middleham tootled her horn at the sharp bend into Church Lane.

She missed the cottage she had felt trapped in for so long. The tiny twisting stairs, her grandmother's chair. Sweetie's imperious yowl.

She missed walking up to the manor, through the village and up the long avenue. Letting herself in the back door, clicking on the coffee machine. Holly and Ben, spreading their homework over the kitchen table. She even missed those stupid dogs.

She missed Max. Oh, how she missed him! Flora felt as if she was tiptoeing around on the edge of a black hole, a bottomless, dark and terrifying chasm.

It was hard now to remember that she had once thought herself in love with Rich. She could look at him and feel nothing but mild surprise that they had ever got together at all. He was still a superlative cook, and wasn't it great to be able to talk about food with someone who wouldn't be just as happy to settle for beans on toast? It was just that there was nothing *else* to talk about with Rich. He was passionate about food, just as she had always been, but when he discussed some of the more elaborate dishes he had in mind to serve, somehow Flora found her mind wandering to the simple smell of a Victoria sponge fresh from the oven.

All that time she had missed the buzz of a restaurant kitchen, she had been learning to enjoy cooking by herself, it seemed. To have the time to make each cake individual and play with the ingredients to find the perfect garnish.

The future yawned in front of her. She had no doubt the restaurant would be successful with Rich at the helm. He was flatteringly keen to persuade her to come on board as a business partner, claiming that her skills as a pastry chef and baker would be the perfect complement to his dazzlingly innovative dishes. She could stay in London and become a celebrated chef. It was what she had always wanted, Flora reminded herself. It was what she still wanted.

Wasn't it?

⋆　⋆　⋆

'When's Flora coming back?' Holly sighed dramatically and threw her school bag onto the kitchen table. 'It's not the same when she's not here.'

It wasn't, Max knew. At least Holly only had to miss her occasionally. He missed her all the time. The first week had stretched to two. She'd sent a polite email telling him that she had 'stuff to sort out' and would be back soon, but she hadn't said when.

The whole house felt empty without her. Every morning Max went into the kitchen and made himself a coffee on that ridiculous machine of hers. He imagined Flora standing next to him, and could almost swear he smelt that light summer scent, feel her warmth. He could almost feel her nudge him out of the way, and roll her eyes, and her smile glimmered so vividly in his mind that he actually turned his head expecting to see her there.

He missed her with a savage ache that took him some time to recognize: the same sickening sense of loss he had felt as a homesick boy, needing to be home. But he had his home, Max tried to convince himself. How could he be home-sick when he was here in the manor?

It was just that it didn't feel like home any more.

Again and again Max reminded him-self of all the reasons why it had been a mistake to get involved with Flora. It hadn't felt like a mistake, though. It had felt absolutely right. But how could he ask her to give up her life and her ambi-tions to live with him? She had been clear from the start that she didn't want to be here. And how could he leave his children and his dogs and try and be part of her life in London? It wouldn't work.

It was just infatuation, Max decided. And great physical chemistry, of course. No wonder he was missing her. But he would meet someone, someday. Someone whose hair smelt of summer and whose mischievous blue eyes were full of sunshine. Someone who could light up a room with her smile, whose warm, lush body could make his senses spin. Someone who could make him laugh and loosen these tight bands around his heart that made it hard to breathe.

Max set his teeth and went through the motions. He sent off a new design and won a new contract. He picked up Holly and Ben and cooked them spaghetti bolognaise, which they hadn't had for so long that they quite enjoyed, although it didn't stop them moaning about the absence of Flora's puddings. He chased up the workmen and arranged for yet another room to be decorated. He studied his bank statements and swore. He walked the dogs and too often found himself walking past Flora's cottage, just in case she had come home, but she never had. She had put the cottage on the market and a FOR SALE sign was already fixed to the wall. It was a pretty little cottage and would sell easily, Max remembered thinking, but even he was taken aback to see a SOLD banner plastered across the sign barely a week after Flora had gone to London.

So this was it. She would be back to cook for Hope's wedding, but then she would go; and once the cottage was sold, there would be no reason for her to come back.

He would just have to accept that and get used to life without her.

Wouldn't he?

'I'm worried about you,' Stella said when he went to pick up the kids at the weekend. 'You're so solitary, Max. You should go out more. There's this girl in my Pilates class who'd be perfect for you — what?' she finished, puzzled, as Max held up a hand.

'I know you're trying to help, Stella, but please don't try and set me up with anyone else.'

Stella looked crushed. 'I only want you to be happy.'

'I know you do,' he said more gently, 'but you're not responsible for my happiness any more. We're divorced. You're the mother of my children, so you'll always be special to me, but who I see and what I do and what makes me happy . . . those things are up to me. There's only one woman who's perfect for me — and she's not in your Pilates class.'

'Flora, I suppose?'

Max nodded. 'Yes, Flora.'

He was responsible for his own happiness — wasn't that what he had told Stella? Max drove home thoughtfully. It was high time he did something about that.

★ ★ ★

It was a soft spring morning, and the plants were almost visibly unfurling in a haze of zingy green. Unable to sleep, Max had got up early to find some solace in gardening. Flora or no Flora, the garden had to be looking its best for Hope's wedding.

Max was nervous. For so long he had been focused on Hasebury Hall and on family obligations, and now he couldn't remember the last time he had taken a risk for himself. His father had been the great risk-taker, and look where that had got him. Max had done better playing safe. But playing safe would not bring Flora back.

On the desk in his study, Max had a ticket to London. He was going to try and get Flora back. He might humiliate himself completely in the process — and probably would — but at least he would know that he had tried.

Ted's ears were pricked, and Bella lifted her head from her paws and gave a little yip. The decorators must have arrived early.

Reluctant to leave the garden, which seemed to be the only place he knew what he was doing, Max headed inside. He needed a word with the painter, anyway. At the back door, he kicked off his boots while the dogs bustled excitedly ahead in the direction of the kitchen. He frowned. The decorators were supposed to be finishing the drawing room, not hanging around in the kitchen. They had finished painting in there.

He whistled for the dogs, but they didn't come. He walked down the passage and pushed open the kitchen door.

And there was Flora, crouched down to make a fuss of the dogs who were both wriggling and moaning with pleasure, their whole bodies wagging.

Max's heart tripped and his mind went dark, blinded by the rush of joy at the sight of her.

She looked up and saw him standing

in the doorway, and when their eyes met, Max felt as if the shackles around his heart had sprung apart to let it float free.

'Hi,' she said with a tentative smile.

'You're back,' he said stupidly.

'Yes.' Flora had rehearsed what she was going to say, but now that she was here and he was just there, her mind was blank. She didn't want to talk, she wanted to throw herself into his arms and beg him to never let her go, but she couldn't do that. She had thought of much better things to say . . . if only she could remember them.

She gave the dogs a final pat and straightened slowly. 'Can you believe I missed them?' she said. 'Do you think I've turned into a dog person after all?'

'Bella and Ted think you've always been a dog person secretly.'

'Maybe they're right. It turns out that I've been a lot of things secretly that I didn't realize before.'

'Oh? Like what?'

'Well, it seems I'm a secret baker, and

would rather make cakes than cook wonderful, innovative dishes.'

'Really?' said Max, moving into the room at last.

'Yes; and also, apparently I'm secretly a country girl, and not a city girl at all.'

A slow smile dawned in his face. 'That's a real shame,' he said. 'Because I've just bought a ticket to London.'

The blue eyes widened in astonishment. 'What on earth for?'

'I thought I might have a go at being a city boy.'

'You can't do that!' Flora stared at him as if he'd lost his mind. 'What about Holly and Ben?'

'I'd have to come back every other weekend, and occasionally during the week, but I can do that.' Max shrugged. 'It's only London, not the other end of the country.'

'But . . . but . . . Bella and Ted would hate London!'

Max came nearer. 'The great thing about dogs, which I think you have to agree makes them superior to cats, is that they just want to be with you. If I'm happy, Bella and Ted will be happy; and I won't be happy without you, Flora.'

Flora put her fingers to a mouth that trembled suddenly. 'Max,' she said unevenly. 'Would you really consider moving to London for me?'

'For my whole life, I've thought of Hasebury Hall as home,' said Max, setting his hands at her waist and looking into eyes that were starry with tears. 'But since you've been gone, I've realized that home isn't a place. It's you.'

'Max,' said Flora. 'Oh, Max. Throw away that ticket. Don't go to London.' She rested her hands on his chest with a tremulous smile. 'I've missed you so much. I only went to London because I thought you wanted me to go, but when I was there, I realized I didn't belong there any more. Maybe I never did. All I could think about was how much I missed it here: the village and this house. And you,' she finished. 'You most of all.'

'I've missed you too,' said Max. 'I spent all my time telling myself to be sensible but it was too late. Somewhere along the line, that stupid pretence for the Crown Princess turned out to be real. I was in love with you before I knew what had happened.'

'You love me?' Flora was dazzled by relief and a dawning happiness. She had come back just wanting a chance to stay a bit longer, and *now*, now he was there and letting go of her waist to cup her face between his palms, and slide his fingers into her hair.

'I do,' he said, dropping kisses over her face. 'I love you, I love you, I love you.' And then he found her mouth and the kiss they shared swept away the misery of the past two weeks in a great whoosh of feeling, tumbling them along in joy and relief.

★ ★ ★

'Are you sure you'll be happy as a country girl?' Max asked her later, when they were sitting on the bench in the herb garden. Flora had made coffee, just like old times, and the dogs were sprawled on the brick patio, making the most of the spring sunshine.

'Completely sure,' said Flora. 'There's only one problem: I've sold the cottage already to a couple who are desperate to move in. It was one of the reasons I came back. The first one was obviously to throw myself at you, and beg you to take me back, which seems to have worked quite well, but I also have to pack up the cottage and need somewhere to put all my things.' She slid a provocative glance at him under her lashes. 'I've inherited all my grandparents' furniture, so I'm really looking for somewhere old and maybe a bit empty . . . '

Max pretended to consider. 'I think I might know just the place,' he said, twining his fingers with hers. 'I could let you move your stuff in here. There's plenty of room, but there *would* be a couple of conditions, I'm afraid.'

'Oh? What sort of conditions.'

'First, you'd need to move in with all your stuff.'

Flora tapped her bottom lip thoughtfully. 'I think I could manage that. What's the second condition?'

'I'm not happy about lying to the Crown Princess,' said Max. 'I think we should make our engagement real, so there's no risk to her seating plans at Hope's wedding.'

'Ooh, does that mean we get to plan a wedding of our own?'

'I was thinking we could elope,' he said, and Flora laughed and kissed him.

'I don't mind what we do, as long as we do it together.'

'So you'll marry me?'

'Of course I will.' Flora sighed happily and leant against him. 'Haven't I had a crush on you since I was fifteen?'

'I thought you were over that?'

'Nope, turns out that I was pretending about that too,' she told him. 'What a relief to stop pretending about everything and just tell the truth!'

'What about your restaurant, Flora?' Max made himself ask. 'I don't want marrying me to mean giving up on your dream.'

'You're my dream, Max.' For once, the blue eyes that looked into his were perfectly serious. 'That crush I had wasn't real, but this is. I still want to cook, of course, but I've realized that I don't want to go back to the pressure of a top kitchen. I want to make simple, delicious food that people really want to eat, and some beautiful cakes for special occasions.'

She gestured to the kitchen garden, bursting with growth, and to the walled garden beyond where the herbaceous borders still needed another few weeks before they were at their spectacular best. 'I thought this would be a perfect place for a garden centre. Why don't you stop sending plants off to die of neglect, and grow plants for gardens in those greenhouses instead? And then I could run a little café that would be a cut above the usual sandwiches and millionaire's shortbread. What do you think?'

Max eyed her with respect. 'I think you might have something there, Moonflower Dreaming. But you've got a royal wedding to cater before you can start planning a café.'

'I know, and I'm keen to get to work,' said Flora. 'I had *such a* good idea for canapes when I was in London. Lucky I'm marrying a man who can give me my fantasy kitchen!'

Max smiled and got up, drawing her to her feet so that he could lead her up to his room. 'Speaking of fantasies . . .' he said.

★　★　★

Three days later, Max staggered into the manor with the last of Flora's belongings from the cottage. Incredibly, the tiny house had produced an immense amount of furniture, pictures and books that were now cluttering up the great hall until a home could be found for it all.

Max had grumbled throughout the

process, of course. 'You can't really want all this rubbish?' he said at regular intervals, but Flora would just pile another box into his arms and tell him not to drop it.

'I know you're just pretending to be grouchy,' she said. 'You can't fool me now. Beneath that crusty exterior, you're a pussycat really.'

'A *pussycat*?' Max pretended outrage. 'I'm a dog man all the way through, as you well know.'

'I think I could convert you to cats,' Flora said. 'In fact, I was thinking it would be nice to have a kitten around the place to keep Ted and Bella in order. We could call it Fluffy or Cuddles or something, so you could enjoy calling for it,' she added with an innocent look.

'Over my dead body!' said Max, but he was fairly sure there would be a kitten ruling the roost before long, whatever he said. He would have to make it up to his dogs somehow.

Now he edged into the hall, a huge

cardboard box in his arms, and negotiated his way through the chairs, empty drawers standing on one end and packing cases oozing bubble wrap. 'This is the last one,' he announced. 'Where do you want it?'

Flora looked up from where she was unwrapping her grandmother's china onto the corner of a table. Bella and Ted were enjoying themselves hugely, pretending there were rats in the discarded balls of scrunched-up news-paper at her feet.

'What's in it?'

'Lead weights, from the feel of it . . . '

She jumped up to open the box and peer inside. 'Granny's recipe books!'

'Great,' sighed Max. 'More cookery books. Just what we needed. I'm going to have to build an extension at this rate. I cannot believe you need all this *stuff*,' he added, looking around the hall, which had once seemed so cold and empty, and remembering how appalled he had been when he had helped Flora carry in all her kitchen equipment the previous November.

'*How* long did you say you were moving in for?' he asked with a mock scowl, and Flora smiled as she leant across the cardboard box to kiss him.

'Forever.'

We do hope that you have enjoyed reading this large print book.

Did you know that all of our titles are available for purchase?

We publish a wide range of high quality large print books including:
Romances, Mysteries, Classics
General Fiction
Non Fiction and Westerns

Special interest titles available in large print are:
The Little Oxford Dictionary
Music Book, Song Book
Hymn Book, Service Book

Also available from us courtesy of Oxford University Press:
Young Readers' Dictionary
(large print edition)
Young Readers' Thesaurus
(large print edition)

For further information or a free brochure, please contact us at:
Ulverscroft Large Print Books Ltd.,
The Green, Bradgate Road, Anstey,
Leicester, LE7 7FU, England.
Tel: (00 44) **0116 236 4325**
Fax: (00 44) **0116 234 0205**

ROMANTIC DOCTOR

Phyllis Mallett

1968: As a doctor at St Jermyn's Hospital, Ann Barling's work is her life, and it seems like romance has passed her by completely. She may as well admit to herself that she's now a confirmed spinster. When she returns to work after a holiday, however, change is afoot in the form of newly hired Dr David Hanbury. He has a reputation, and seems determined to add Ann to his list of conquests. But she's having none of it . . .

CHRISTMAS AT COORAH CREEK

Janet Gover

English nurse Katie Brooks is spending Christmas at Coorah Creek. She was certain that leaving London was the right decision, but her new job in the outback is more challenging than she ever imagined. Scott Collins rescued her on her first day and has been a source of comfort ever since. But he no longer calls the town home — it's too full of bad memories, and he doesn't plan on sticking around long. Scott needs to leave. Katie needs to stay. They have until Christmas to decide their future . . .

THE CHRISTMAS CHOIR

Jo Bartlett

After a chance encounter with a young homeless man, high-flyer Anna reassesses her life. Handing in her notice at her City job, she returns home to St Nicholas Bay. There, she finds that the new vicar is none other than Jamie: the man who severed their relationship when they were teenagers, and took off abroad alone. The pair renew their old acquaintanceship — just as friends. But are the sparks of their long-ago love kindling into life once more?

JESSICA'S CHRISTMAS KISS

Alison May

When Jessica was fifteen, she shared a magical kiss with a mystery boy at a Christmas party. Now almost thirty, she is faced with a less than magical Christmas after uncovering her husband's secret affair. And, whilst she wouldn't admit it, she sometimes finds herself thinking about that perfect Christmas kiss, back when her life still seemed full of hope and possibility. But she never would have guessed that the boy she kissed in the kitchen all those years ago might still think about her too . . .

TWO LOVES

Denise Robins

Bill is handsome, tender and exciting, but Cherry knows she can't live on love alone. Phillip doesn't attract her like Bill does, but his wealth can buy her everything she's always wanted. Cherry is determined to have them both. Cleverly concealing one's existence from the other, she begins leading a dangerous double life, unknowingly pushing all three of them towards disaster . . .